Love is
a time of enchantment:
in it all days are fair and all fields
green. Youth is blest by it,
old age made benign: the eyes of love see
roses blooming in December,
and sunshine through rain. Verily
is the time of true-love
a time of enchantment — and
Oh! how eager is woman
to be bewitched!

HIGHLAND DESTINY

Soon after the battle of Naseby the Emreys were forced into exile, and in Scotland Sir John Emrey and his sister become involved in the turbulent affairs of the Macdonalds. Blanche becomes a confidente of Fiona, a young Macdonald chieftain who is menaced on all sides. Her cousin Alexander, handsome, debonair, puzzling. Is he Fiona's friend or enemy? Does he love her, or desire marriage for the position it will give him? Fiona wants none of them, and Blanche cares more than she wishes to admit.

MARINA OLIVER

HIGHLAND DESTINY

Complete and Unabridged

ULVERSCROFT
Leicester

First published in Great Britain in 1979 by
Robert Hale Limited
London

First Large Print Edition
published April 1991

British Library CIP Data

Oliver, Marina *1934* –
Highland destiny. – Large print ed. –
Ulverscroft large print series: romance
I. Title
823.914 [F]

ISBN 0–7089–2411–5

Published by
F. A. Thorpe (Publishing) Ltd.
Anstey, Leicestershire
Set by Words & Graphics Ltd.
Anstey, Leicestershire
Printed and bound in Great Britain by
T. J. Press (Padstow) Ltd., Padstow, Cornwall

1

BLANCHE walked briskly down the hillside despite the fierce heat of the noon sun, swinging her basket and aglow with pleasure at having performed a task well. Smiling, she compared the praises of old Lizzie Smith, from whose tiny cottage she had just come, with the charges of hoydenish behaviour that her governess too often levelled at her. Old Lizzie, once a servant at the Manor, had greatly appreciated her visit, and Blanche, impatient to be thought fully grown, was aware that by encouraging her to perform more of such tasks her mother was recognizing her maturity. Lady Emrey had issued many warnings, though, about not straying from the track and returning home immediately, for one never knew when one might be surprised by troops of soldiers, and Blanche had seen enough of the war to realize that her mother's fears were not unfounded. In these troubled times it was but common sense to take precautions.

The track twisted down between high banks, and as Blanche turned the last sharp corner the long, low stone house that was her home appeared before her, basking in the sunshine. Beside the doorway she saw several men surrounding a litter from which someone was being lifted gently and then carried into the house. Fear clutched at Blanche's heart, and after a moment's horrified pause when she recalled in all its vivid detail a similar scene one year earlier, in 1644, when her dead father had been carried home from Marston Moor, she was racing down the last slope, her skirts held high, all thoughts of her new dignity forgotten.

"Oh God! Please God, let it not be John!" she prayed as she ran, thinking less of her own loss if her adored brother were hurt or killed, but of the devastating blow it would be to her mother, who had been so shocked and ill after the death of her father. If John were gone too her mother would be inconsolable.

Breathless, Blanche tore under the stone gateway and along the short drive that led between neatly tended flowerbeds to the house. Heedless of the curious stares cast at her, she quickly scanned the faces of the men who stood around, but John was not amongst them. The litter had been removed and its occupant was inside the house. Blanche ran on towards the door, distraught, and the men moved aside to permit her to pass. Just as she reached the wide, low steps her brother appeared at the top, and gasping with relief Blanche flung herself towards him. He caught her to him, hugging her closely while she stammered out her fears.

"Be calm, child!" he admonished, and turned to thank the men, saying that refreshments were being prepared for them in the kitchens. Nodding, they moved away round the house and John held Blanche away from him, looking down at her gently.

"I was so terrified!" she explained. "It was so like when — when father was brought home, and I feared for you!"

"I am unscathed," he answered sombrely, "but there was a disastrous battle and many were hurt. A good friend of mine was sorely wounded and since he could travel no further on his way home to Scotland I brought him here. Now, will you show

3

that you are a soldier's daughter and help the maids feed my men? Can you do that after the fright you have received? I must go to see if there is aught I can do to aid mother in settling Angus."

Blanche drew herself away, smiled at him a little tremulously, and nodded, then turned to go into the vast kitchen where two of the maids were hurriedly arranging pies, bread and cheese, and a huge sirloin of beef on the big centre table. Blanche went to collect mugs and set these out, then filled them with ale from a huge blackjack. The men, almost a dozen of them, came in and seated themselves, smiling and jesting with the girls although they eyed Blanche herself with some wariness. She was longing to discover what had occurred, and when they appeared to have satisfied their first pangs of hunger she began to ask questions.

One of the oldest amongst them constituted himself their spokesman.

"'Twere near Market Harborough, Missee," he said heavily, "a place called Naseby, I 'eard say. We was outnumbered, an' they devils surrounded us!" He paused, drained his mug, then wiped his hand over his lips. Sighing, he shook his head mournfully. "It shouldn't ha' been! If only the Prince 'ad come back after the first charge! Or the King brought up the reserve instead o' riding away when they was needed!"

"Is the King's army beaten utterly?" Blanche asked in dismay.

"'Twould seem so. Aye, all's lost, and we need to save what we can for ourselves!"

"But who is this man you have brought here?"

"A Scot, a friend o' Sir John, Missee. 'E were wounded, bad, but 'e would ride northwards until 'e lost too much blood and Sir John persuaded 'im to come 'ere to be tended."

"I see. Were many wounded?" Blanche asked fearfully.

"Too many! Or taken!" another, younger man, put in. "The Ironsides, damn them to hell, put even the women following the army to the sword! An' the rest are fled. The King'll never get another army now!"

Gloomily they discussed the disaster, and Blanche listened in growing dismay. The King was in dire trouble, it seemed, if his army really had been broken to pieces.

They were not left long in fruitless discussion. John soon appeared and, with an approving glance at his sister, briskly thanked the men for their help and handed each of them a coin.

"The King will no doubt be gathering his forces together. I look to seeing you all again soon, when we'll show these New Model men they're not the only ones that can fight!"

They looked dubious, but with many expressions of thanks to Blanche and the maids, the soldiers gathered up their belongings and departed. John went to see them on their way, and then returned to the kitchen where Blanche was helping to clear away the remnants of the meal.

"Leave that and come and talk with me," he said to her. 'Tis months since I was home."

Eagerly plying him with questions, Blanche accompanied him to a small but sunny parlour.

"Who is your friend? Should you not be with him?"

"Mother is caring for him, and will do

all that is possible. I fear, though, that there is little she can do. He lost a great deal of blood from several wounds."

"Poor man," Blanche said softly. "He is your friend?"

"Yes. He is Angus Macdonald, a Scot from the Western Highlands. He came to England with Prince Rupert, for they had fought together as boys in Germany. We have for some time been companions."

They remained silent for a time, then, making an effort to shake off his melancholy, John began asking Blanche questions about her own doings, and what had been happening at home during the months he had been away. Proudly she related all the work she had been doing, saying that now her mother relied on her a great deal. John smiled, thinking how lovely she looked when animated, her huge dark eyes sparkling and her black, unruly curls tumbling about her piquant face. Though only just fourteen Blanche was already a beauty, and as she matured she would be very desirable. But what would be her future in this uncertain world, he wondered bleakly. The man she had been promised to several years earlier had died shortly before their own father, and he, now her guardian, had been too preoccupied with the fighting to make any other arrangements for her. He must now consider it, he realized, and ask his mother whether she had any suitable man in mind.

Blanche's pleasure in her brother's company was scarcely dimmed by the knowledge that a man lay upstairs desperately ill, for she was permitted no part in the nursing of him. For two days he clung to life but then, having recovered consciousness for a few hours, he quietly died. John had been with him for these last lucid hours, but when it was all over he came out of the bedroom carrying a heavy jewelled sword, and shut himself away in the room where his father had dealt with the business of the estate.

That evening after supper John broached the problem of Blanche's future to his mother.

"There are no suitable young men in the district," Lady Emrey said worriedly. "I have been thinking long about this, for your father had no close kinsfolk, and mine are far away in Ulster, and she would need protection if — if aught befell you and me."

John laid his hand briefly on her shoulder. "We must make plans. What of Robert Petherick? He is from a wealthy family and of good birth."

"He has joined Parliament, and his younger brother was killed a few months back," Lady Emrey explained. "They have all been killed or have joined Parliament or their families are against the King. That, or they are Papists. I could not permit Blanche to wed into either a Papist or a Parliamentarian family!"

"No, indeed. Well, if there is no-one suitable hereabouts, we must seek further from home. I have many friends in the army, of course, but life is so uncertain for us all that will scarce serve. Had father no kinsfolk? I thought there was a cousin?"

"There is only a second cousin, a Charles Askew, and I have not heard from him in years."

"He lives near Durham, does he not? I will pay him a visit and enquire whether he knows of anyone suitable. Blanche is young, and decidedly pretty, and will have a substantial dowry. She's a good match for any man."

Lady Emrey sighed. "I would I could keep her with me for company. She is young yet."

"Indeed, but a betrothal would safeguard her. We must not delay, though she is certainly too young as yet to wed."

He fell silent, gazing into the embers of the small fire which had been lit, for even in this hot June the evenings could become chilly. Lady Emrey watched him, thinking fondly how like his father he had become, and sorrowing at the disruption the war had brought to his life. Although he was a good soldier she knew that his heart was not in it, and he would rather be caring for his lands and raising his own family.

"Have you no wedding plans for yourself?" she asked gently. "Has no girl taken your fancy?"

He grinned briefly. "Oh, as to that — I've seen no-one to tempt me! There's no leisure for me to think of marrying until we are safe. When that happens I'll lose no time, I promise you, in finding a suitable wife and giving you a grandchild! There's too much else to do yet. I will set off for Durham tomorrow and attempt to settle

Blanche's future. Afterwards, I promised Angus that I would go and tell his father of his death, and take back his sword. It is apparently much venerated in his clan. By that time, mayhap, the King's armies will have gathered together again and I can rejoin him to make another push to end this war. For the moment my duties towards Blanche and Angus are more urgent."

He departed on the following day, and Blanche awaited his return with some trepidation. Despite her desire to be adult, the knowledge that he intended to arrange a betrothal for her perturbed her. She did not wish to leave her home, married to some stranger, but she knew that it would be childish as well as useless to protest. She must marry, and she knew that John and her mother would choose a man that she could like and respect. She could only hope that there would be plenty of opportunity for her to meet and come to know the man before she had to be married to him.

John would be gone for about a week. Two days after his departure, early in the morning, Blanche was in the schoolroom at the back of the house with her governess, Mistress Evans, when they heard a loud knock at the door and officious shouts demanding to know who was at home.

Ignoring Mistress Evans' anguished plea for decorum, Blanche pulled open the door and ran along to the top of the stairs. Below her in the large, stone-flagged hall her mother stood proudly confronting a couple of soldiers, Parliament men by the looks of their severely plain dress and close-cropped hair.

"Where is the traitor John Emrey?" one of them was demanding stridently.

"Sir John, my son, is away from home," Lady Emrey retorted with spirit. "What is the meaning of this unmannerly intrusion?"

One of the men, the taller, took a step towards her and Blanche, with a cry of anger, sprang down the stairs and stood protectively beside her mother. The soldier turned and looked her up and down insolently, a smile spreading slowly over his harsh features.

"A tasty morsel, hey, Thomas? Young, but tender, no doubt."

"Blanche, go back upstairs immediately!" Lady Emrey commanded urgently.

"Not so fast, my good woman. Who is this?"

"By what right do you burst in here and question me so?"

He touched his sword and cocked an eyebrow at her, but she did not flinch. "Answer me, woman, or you'll rue it!"

"My name is Blanche Emrey. Who are you? And why are you here trying to bully us?" Blanche said swiftly, angrily, before her mother could reply.

"Oho, complaisant too! We do well, Thomas! Mistress Blanche," bowing ironically, "we are come to requisition quarters for our troops who will be coming this way tonight, and this house is suitable."

"What is your authority?" Lady Emrey asked, suppressing her anger.

Again he indicated his sword. "God, Parliament, and the King!" he proclaimed loudly.

"God chooses strange companions in this Parliament," Lady Emrey commented acidly, "and the King's wishes run counter to those of the rebels! You can scarce act for both!"

"Be silent! I am not here to dispute with ignorant women! The men will arrive before supper. You will remain here to ensure that all is provided fittingly. I will return soon. I beg you, Mistress Blanche, to do me the honour of supping with me!"

He bowed to her while his companion, hitherto a silent spectator, sniggered.

"I wish for nought to do with traitors to the King!" Blanche replied scornfully.

"You'll sing a different tune by morning, I'll warrant," was the only reply, flung over the man's shoulder as he turned and strode from the house.

Lady Emrey sank onto a stool before the huge fireplace pulling Blanche down to kneel beside her. She put her arms comfortingly about the girl.

"Do they mean it?" Blanche asked quietly.

"Indeed they do. We have been fortunate to evade such a visitation earlier, but we are somewhat remote in these northern hills."

"Can we not fight them — barricade the house?" Blanche asked.

Lady Emrey shook her head sadly.

"We have not enough men, for only the very young or old servants are left to us; the rest have gone off to fight. No, we can do nought to save the house from them, but we must not stay! I must hide you, for that villain's intentions were plain enough!"

Blanche shivered. "Where can we go?"

Lady Emrey was thinking. "I will send Mistress Evans and the servants away. They can go to their homes, or to friends, and it will be thought we go with them. We will seek shelter with Lizzie for a few days. I trust that they will pass on soon, and we can return."

"Yes, Lizzie's cottage is well-hidden, and she will willingly give us shelter."

Swiftly Lady Emrey organised the servants. They were all sent away except for William, the old coachman. He buried the most valuable of the plate beneath a stone flag in the cellar while Blanche and Lady Emrey made bundles for themselves of their plainest gowns, and sewed their jewels into pouches to wear on belts round their waists.

"We must pass as villagers if necessary," Lady Emrey explained.

"They might wreck the house! Cannot we hide more?" Blanche asked, distressed.

"I dare not hide too much, for then they would suspect and search. As it is they might be content with what we leave them. Let us hope so. Come, we will pack all the food we can into panniers. If we turn all the horses loose they will graze on the hillsides, but first we will lead the packponies up to Lizzie's cottage with what food we can take, or she could not feed us."

Swiftly they worked, packing vegetables, flour, salt, eggs, the remains of joints and cooked pies, with other provisions, into panniers. Lady Emrey added some preserves and medicines from her still-room, and a few bottles of wine. William hoisted two casks of ale onto one of the ponies, added two mattresses and bundles of blankets, and eventually they were ready. At the last moment Blanche remembered the sword of Angus Macdonald and ran back to rescue it from the small room where John had placed it.

Dressed in an old grey gown she had almost outgrown, Blanche led the way from the stableyard and through the kitchen garden. She guided the leading pony, and keeping close beside the hedge that hid them from the sight of anyone watching the front of the house, went towards a belt of trees that gave them further cover.

They gained the shelter of one of the steep paths that wound between high banks towards the upper hills, and had soon reached Lizzie's cottage. There had been no time to warn her, and she exclaimed in dismay at their story, bustling round to unload their provisions and make room in her tiny cottage for them. William took the ponies, promising to hide the panniers in a small cave not far away where they would be undiscovered, and then turn the ponies loose before departing for his daughter's home some miles distant across the hills.

The next few days were strange, and for Blanche, exciting. She had never imagined what it would be like to live entirely in one room, with only a small loft, reached by a ladder, which Lizzie insisted she and her mother used to sleep in.

"Ye'll be safer, my lady, apart from more comfortable," she insisted, and indeed there was no space to lay out three beds in the downstairs room.

Every morning and evening Blanche walked to a spot where she could look down on the Manor and reported that the soldiers appeared to be in no haste to move on.

"What if John returns, unaware of their presence?" she asked on the third day. "He'd walk straight into a trap! Mayhap they are waiting for him!"

"Do not fear, Blanche. William promised to watch for him. His daughter lives on the road John must take. I've no doubt William will warn him and tell him where to find us."

Satisfied, Blanche returned to her task of helping Lizzie cook an appetizing stew made from rabbit and wild herbs, eagerly asking the old woman what uses the herbs were put to.

John arrived as it was growing dusk three days later, anxious and furiously angry. Once satisfied that they had not been harmed, he was for storming straight into the Manor to confront the occupants, and was only dissuaded when Lady Emrey pointed out that then the soldiers would be bound to discover Blanche's hiding place.

"Then I'll go and see the Hector, Mr Henderson. I'll not be seen, for 'tis dark and moonless. He'll tell me what is happening."

He departed, to return an hour later with disquieting news.

"The house and all its contents are

confiscated by order of Parliament," he told his mother and sister. "I am looked for, with a substantial reward offered, and the leader of the troop has been boasting at the inn of what he'll do when he discovers Blanche. It seems he has been preoccupied until now, but means to begin a wider search for her tomorrow."

"John, he's a devil! She must not fall into his hands!"

"Indeed not, Mother! We must leave here early tomorrow."

"Where can we go? Did you have any success with Mr Askew? Could we go to him?"

"No, I fear not. He died a year back of smallpox, and leaves no family. We will have to go to Ireland, and when I have seen you safely with your people, Mother, I will return to avenge this insult."

They were discussing the best way to take when Blanche remembered the sword and withdrew it from its hiding place behind a roughly carved settle.

"You must take this to Scotland," she reminded John. "Had you forgot?"

John stared at her. "You saved it? My dear, I am so grateful. I have been puzzling how I might retrieve it, for I had sworn to Angus that I would return it to his family. It gives me an idea. His father is one of the Macdonald chieftains on the mainland, and from there and with his help we could travel through the Isles, also ruled by Macdonalds, to Ireland."

2

EARLY on the following day they set off. John had been able to catch one of the ponies grazing nearby, and Blanche rode this while Lady Emrey rode pillion behind her son. Later, he hoped to catch better horses for them, for several that they had turned loose were still roaming in the hills.

The journey through the most northerly parts of England and far into the central Highlands was long and arduous, despite the better mounts they soon obtained, and sometimes it was dangerous. Some of Lady Emrey's jewels were sold to enable them to buy saddles and bridles, warm cloaks, and food. They sheltered at small inns or cottages, and once beneath a haystack when they were far from human habitation. It was more than two weeks before they reached their destination, for they had to travel by the less frequented roads and keep a constant watch for roving bands of soldiers.

"A year since we might not have been able to cross the border," John explained, "for the Covenanters guarded every mile. Now, most fortunately for us, they are kept occupied by Montrose. Since he changed sides to support the King he has inflicted some severe defeats on them, aided, incidentally, by the Macdonalds. They follow some of the Irish clan who came over to his support."

As they passed from the rolling hills of the Lowlands into the more rugged mountains the way grew more hazardous, and they frequently came across people who spoke no English. They made progress, however, and once they entered the Macdonald lands John obtained swift and efficient guidance by showing the sword he carried and explaining that he brought it to the chieftain.

They arrived at their destination late one evening, to find the many-turreted castle, silhouetted against the rose and orange streaks of the setting sun, perched on top of a rocky promontory that fell sheer on two sides to a wide loch that curved around it in a crescent shape, enfolding it protectively. On the landward sides there was a huddle of grey stone houses with turf roofs, enclosed by a rough wall that went right into the waters of the loch. A few houses sprawled outside the main gateway in the centre of the wall, but several of these looked derelict, and none appeared to be inhabited. Dominating the little town, set proudly on the hill behind the wall, was the castle, its entrance consisting of twin grey stone towers, dwarfed by the massive keep built right on the summit of the hill.

Lady Emrey was near exhaustion, and smiled weakly at Blanche as they passed through the little town, across the market place in front of a squat stone church, and towards the castle. John hammered on the gate and a small grill was uncovered from within.

"Who is it?" a gruff voice demanded, and John held up Angus' sword.

"I bring the sword of the Macdonalds to its home! Conduct me to your chieftain!" he announced, and the man stared at him in surprise, then turned to confer with a hidden companion. He reappeared, nodded, and the gate creaked open. John led the way into the large inner courtyard and dismounted, turning to lift Lady

Emrey down. Blanche slid out of her saddle and stood looking about her in awe. She had never seen so magnificent a fortress.

A man, tall and powerfully built, appeared on the steps before the main entrance to the castle and looked down on them. He walked slowly down the steps, gazing steadily at the sword John held.

"Greetings, strangers," he said quietly. "I am Hugh Macdonald. I understand you have something for me. I beg you to come with me."

He gave his arm to Lady Emrey, whom John introduced, and then turned to lead the way through the vast doorway, across a high, vaulted, stone-walled hall, and through into a smaller apartment, comfortably furnished with tapestries and upholstered chairs. He led Lady Emrey to one of them, and indicated that Blanche took another, then he turned to John.

"You have, it would seem, grievous news — of my son?"

John bowed his head. "Indeed, I fear so, Lord Hugh."

Quietly he told the bereaved father of his son's death after the battle of Naseby, and described Angus' last few hours, repeating his messages for his family. Lord Hugh listened courteously, no emotion visible on his face apart from a certain tautness about his mouth.

When John had finished he stepped across the small room holding out the sword, and Lord Hugh received it from him.

"I thank you, for your friendship with Angus, and this last sign of it you have offered him. I will have rooms prepared for you and the ladies."

He clapped his hands and a small, wiry man appeared from an inner room. Sir Hugh spoke swiftly in Gaelic and the man nodded and waited.

"Davie will conduct you to your rooms. I will see you at supper in a short while. I must go to my daughter first."

Admiring his courtesy amidst his grief, they left him and followed the little man Davie up some steep, winding stairs. He led them to small bedchambers, comfortable but oddly shaped, for they were on the outer wall of the keep, their narrow windows overlooking the loch through thick, solid walls.

Blanche's room connected with her mother's, and John was on the other side. Davie, who spoke English with a thick accent, said that maids would bring hot water immediately.

"Is there aught else ye need? Ask me if so, and I'll fetch or send for it," he told them. "I'll wait outside and take ye down to the hall for supper."

Thankfully they washed, removing the travel stains, and changed into fresh gowns. As Blanche finished brushing back her hair, weird sounds came to her, apparently from just outside the window, wailing, painful sounds.

"What is it?" she called to her mother.

"The pipes, child. 'Tis a custom here, when there is a death, to pipe a lament."

Blanche listened to the wild, eerie music, and found it extraordinarily difficult to prevent her own tears from flowing as the agony and longing in the sound penetrated her mind.

As it finished with a dwindling wail Davie and John appeared and the Emreys followed the little man, somewhat reluctantly, to join Lord Hugh in the hall.

He came forward to greet them, then led

them over to present them to his daughter, a girl of Blanche's age.

"Fiona will see to your comforts, Mistress Blanche," he said, and the girl bowed her head gravely. She was slightly taller than Blanche, with long blond hair and deep blue eyes. She was not a beauty, but there was a quality of quiet confidence about her, and her chin was raised in an attitude of determination that was most attractive. She was composed, but there was a suspicious brightness in her eyes. However, her voice was steady as she murmured greetings and John, studying his friend's sister with compassion, felt a surge of admiration for her courage.

After the first few minutes conversation was restricted, for the two pipers entered the hall, their plaids of soft reds and greens pleated and belted round their waists while the ends were flung over their shoulders. They played their lament throughout the meal, marching up and down the length of the hall. Fiona made some pretence of eating, but Blanche, full of sympathy for the bereaved girl, was herself unable to swallow more than a few morsels of food.

At last the meal was over, and Lady

Emrey tactfully pleaded exhaustion and carried Blanche off to bed, leaving Lord Hugh and Fiona with John, for Lord Hugh had asked John to tell Fiona himself of her brother's messages.

"She bore it so bravely," he later told his mother. "For so young a girl, but a few months older than Blanche, she showed great powers of self-control. Angus was proud of his sister, but I did not think she had such a noble courage!"

Lady Emrey was to judge that herself, for on the day following their arrival at the castle Fiona sought her out to talk with her about her brother.

"You tended him at the last, and I hope you will tell me of him," she said simply.

That evening at supper Lord Hugh asked what the Emreys' plans were, and John explained that he intended to escort his mother and sister to Ireland before rejoining the King.

"Ireland? Your relatives are Catholics?"

"No. My family came from Cheshire and my great-uncle, a younger son, settled near Belfast when he was a young man," Lady Emrey explained. "As the rest of my grandfather's branch of the family are dead, they are now my only kin."

"I think Ireland is unsafe. The Confederates are not sending aid to His Majesty, despite his dire need. The Earl of Ormond cannot persuade them, for they demand the return of cathedrals, and freedom to practise their faith. They will turn against the Protestants soon."

"The King's cause appears lost," John said gloomily. "Have you heard news out of England?"

"Aye, and bad news. Carlisle has fallen, and Pomfret and Scarborough surrendered. It is only from Montrose that help can come."

"He is still successful?"

"Undoubtedly. He plans now to march southwards, to invade the Lowlands. Why do you not join him, Sir John? You'd serve the King best that way, by swelling a victorious army."

"It is something to be considered. I may return after escorting my mother and Blanche to Ireland."

"As to that, I have another proposal. I do not relish the thought of sending you on to Ireland in its present unsettled state. Will you remain here and bear my daughter company?"

Lady Emrey looked at him in astonishment. "You are generous, Lord Hugh!"

He smiled sadly. "Not so. Fiona needs a woman's guidance, more so as she is now my heir. I had intended, later, sending her to my brother's wife, but she must begin to learn about my lands. Besides, she has taken a liking to you and your daughter, and your companionship would help her recover from her loss."

After more discussion Lady Emrey agreed that it would be the best plan. She did not know her cousins in Ireland, and Lord Hugh's warnings of unrest there disturbed her. Here in this Highland fastness they would be safe, and in close touch with John when he joined the Marquis of Montrose. Blanche was delighted with what she had seen of the castle and heartily approved of the plan. The next day at breakfast Fiona asked whether they would like her to conduct them on a tour of the castle. John was eager to ride away to join Montrose, but willingly agreed to postpone his departure until the following morning.

Fiona smiled at Blanche. "I am glad that you are staying so that I shall not have to go to Aunt Katriona. Father says that we may study together, and I shall enjoy having a companion at my lessons. But now I want to show you the castle. It is a rambling place, for our ancestors have frequently added to it in the past few hundred years, even building a maze of rooms in the rock below. I expect it will take time for you to learn your way about. Let us go down this way, then we can walk along the loch terrace, which gives a wonderful view of the surroundings."

Chatting composedly, showing no hint of her grief for her brother apart from a grave, unsmiling countenance, she led the way. Blanche gasped as they came out onto the terrace, for spreading before them and stretching for miles was a wild, mountainous country, the lower slopes of the hills covered with forests, while the loch spread away on either side, the eastern part winding through the hills, while to the south it gradually widened as it neared the sea. Leaning over the wall she saw the sheer, dizzy drop to the water, making the castle impregnable on two sides. Fiona led the way up onto the battlements of the keep so that they could see on the other side the little town sprawling down the slopes of the hill and around its foot. A rough wall enclosed most of the town, apart from the few houses they had seen, apparently abandoned, outside. Blanche asked why none of them seemed to be occupied.

"The people are afraid to live outside now," Fiona explained. "Since the troubles with the Covenant there has been much lawlessness and we have suffered, for our enemies take the opportunity of raiding us for cattle and whatever else they can steal. The Campbells especially have been troublesome since Inverary Castle, the main stronghold of Argyle, their chief, was burned by Montrose last winter. There were many Macdonalds with him, you see, and the Campbells want revenge. We are uncomfortably close to Campbell lands."

The two girls soon struck up a firm friendship and spent nearly all their time together. Lady Emrey busied herself, at Lord Hugh's request, with the welfare of his people, and John was away with Montrose's army.

He was in time to join the Marquis' gallant attempt to restore the King's fortunes by marching southwards, and fought in the victorious battle at Kilsyth in mid August, then marched on to occupy Glasgow.

It was the pinnacle of Montrose's achievement. In a year he had formed an army from nothing, fought and won six battles with the loss of barely a couple of hundred men, and after each had been compelled to recruit again as his Highlanders drifted back homewards with the cattle they had seized as prizes, this representing all the pay they could expect and the livelihood of their families. All but one of the Covenant's armies were broken, but that one under David Leslie returned in September and inflicted on Montrose his first defeat.

John came with the news.

"We were surprised in our camp at Philiphaugh, early in the morning," he explained grimly. "Alistair Macdonald and his Irish were not with us, and their absence proved disastrous. Our horses were still grazing and we could not reach them. Most of us, indeed, were still in Selkirk. The Douglas band fled, leaving it to the rest to mount a defence. Poor devils! They were butchered, even those who surrendered on promise of quarter were afterwards lined up in rows and shot. Leslie ordered the women to be slaughtered, hacked to pieces, and those who survived were taken to Linlithgow and thrown into the river."

"How do you know this?" Blanche asked, horrified.

"A few escaped. Montrose himself had to be dragged from the field. At first he was disheartened, wishing he had perished with the others, but now he plans to raise another army. His name alone is worth an army to the King. I have come to ask your men to help yet again, Lord Hugh."

More men were recruited, and Montrose tried to regain the initiative. The astounding news that Prince Rupert had surrendered Bristol to the Roundheads came, then a message that Digby was coming north to meet Montrose on the border.

This plan failed, and Digby fled to the Isle of Man. There was no longer any hope of reinforcements from England.

Through the long, cold, northern winter the struggle continued to raise an army, from chiefs quarrelling amongst themselves and unwilling to redeem their promises. The main defector was Huntly, who was madly jealous of Montrose, and who wavered, finally rejecting the orders he received. The Gordons were lost to the cause, but almost immediately the final blow fell when the news came that King Charles had given himself up to a Scottish army in England and ordered Montrose to disband his army and himself go to France.

John, having come to admire Montrose intensely in the few short months he had known him, was bitter when he returned to the castle.

"He is betrayed! He has lost everything, and now this!"

"What do you intend to do now?" Lord Hugh asked calmly.

John shook his head despondently. "I cannot tell. The war would seem to be over. I might join the Marquis — he escaped to Norway — but I have not thought fully on it."

"I need a steward. Remain here. Oh, you would be free to go, with my blessing, if there is any future possibility of supporting the King, but for the moment you have no such hope. I am getting old and could employ you here. Will you accept?"

"It is a surprising offer, my lord," John replied.

"Think about it. Discuss it with your mother. She would like to see more of you, I have no doubt."

Lady Emrey was in favour of the plan, pointing out that Fiona was still too young to take over much of the management of her father's lands, and Lord Hugh was partly crippled with gout.

"He needs an active man to ride about and supervise his lands, and has no-one in his family. His nephews are all too young, save one who has his own lands to manage."

"I have met him," John answered. "Alexander Macdonald was with Montrose and has gone with him to Norway. He sent his — regards to Fiona," he added slowly, and Lady Emrey cast him a swift, appraising look.

"What manner of man is he?" she asked casually.

"Very high and mighty!" John declared. "A good fighter, but somewhat haughty. He asked many questions as to our being here, and wanted to know if Fiona's betrothal

36

was concluded. I did not know aught of the matter."

"Lord Hugh has told me she is to wed a Crawford from the Borders. It was arranged long ago. But will you accept his offer?"

John did so, and began to assist Lord Hugh and Fiona. For the Emreys the next two years were pleasant, despite their dismay at events in England where the King, betrayed and handed over to the English Parliamentary Commissioners by the Scots, did not appear to be in a happy situation.

Mr Henderson, the Rector at their old home, wrote occasionally with news, and they heard that the Manor had been given to a Roundhead soldier from Lincolnshire who had fought with Cromwell. All their old neighbours, whatever their private convictions, were forced to comply with the new rulers. The Emreys had to abandon for the time being any hope of recovering what had been lost, or of returning to their old home. They settled down with the Macdonalds and came to love the Highlands, so different from what they had been accustomed to.

Then, soon after Blanche's seventeenth

birthday, Lord Hugh fell ill and late in July in the year 1648 he died peacefully in his sleep. For a day Fiona was prostrate with grief, gently cosseted by her old nurse Janet, but on the next morning she appeared, pale and dry-eyed, to take over her duties as chieftain. Only when she was alone with Janet or Blanche did she allow her grief to overwhelm her. Elsewhere she dealt competently with affairs as she had been training to do since the death of Angus, calmly issuing orders for her father's funeral and greeting the guests who arrived to pay their respects.

Amongst the first of these was her uncle Colin, the next eldest brother of her father. Blanche had not met him before since the brothers had done their utmost to avoid contact with one another, and was struck by his total dissimilarity to Lord Hugh. Colin was a small man, with shifty eyes and a weak mouth, always too ready to agree with whatever was said, but showing signs of querulousness if his will were thwarted. With him came his wife, Katriona, who made up for her husband's vacillations by an aggressive manner and a complete disregard for anyone else's comfort.

"Well, niece, we have seen little enough of you since the death of your brother, but now we will be here to help you," Katriona announced.

"I have been busy, as you can imagine, learning to take Angus' place," Fiona replied smoothly. "How are your children? I long especially to see my god-daughter, Margaret."

"We will send for her as soon as this business is over. She is four, and a lively miss. She will keep you from pining while your uncle sorts out matters."

Fiona's lips tightened, but she did not reply, merely nodding and turning to Lady Emrey who waited nearby, to desire her to show the Lady Katriona to the rooms that had been prepared for her.

As Katriona swept from the hall Fiona turned with a rueful smile to Blanche.

"I foresee trouble until I can convince her that I am now chieftain, and not she through her husband," she said, laughing slightly. "My aunt has always resented the fact that Colin was the second son!"

She had no more time to discuss it, for another guest arrived. He was a dark, swarthy man, slightly above middle height, but broad and muscular, a powerfully built man. Blanche judged him to be in his mid thirties. He was clad in green and blue trews, and strode confidently into the room, casting a quick glance about him before bowing low over Fiona's hand. Standing before her, he regarded her intently from eyes set close together above a hooked nose.

"Welcome, my Lord Campbell."

"Dear child! A lamentable occasion, in truth, but I see that you are bearing up bravely. If it becomes too much of a strain, rely on me! It shall never be said that Duncan Campbell was remiss in helping his neighbour at such a sad time. Our past differences shall all be forgotten, for they were quarrels of our forebears, were they not, and not of our making!"

Fiona murmured suitable replies to his effusive remarks, and Blanche realised that he was a neighbouring chieftain. She had taken an instant dislike to him, and could see from the way Fiona reacted to him that she was uncomfortable in his presence. Both girls breathed a sigh of relief when he took himself off.

Late that night Fiona came to Blanche's room.

"Do you mind if we talk?" she asked, pausing by the door. "I cannot sleep."

The funeral was due to take place on the following day, and Blanche was well aware of the strain her friend was under. She moved over and patted the bed beside her.

"Get under the covers or you will be cold. Even in mid summer the Highland nights are chill."

Gratefully Fiona slid into the bed, and sat for a while hugging her knees. "What do you think of my family?" she asked abruptly.

"I have not yet sorted them all out. Your Uncle Colin I know, but did not your father have another brother? It is not the Uncle Bruce who arrived late tonight, is it?"

"No. Bruce Maclean is my mother's brother. Father's youngest brother was David, but he died fighting in Germany, at Lützen, where King Gustavus Adolphus himself was slain. He has a son, Alexander, but he is with Montrose, I believe, and I doubt if he has yet even heard of my father's death, and is unlikely to come.

He is the best of them all, and though he is sometimes overbearing I could wish him here. What do you think of Black Duncan?" she asked abruptly.

"I would not trust him a yard, if that!" Blanche declared roundly. "He made me shiver, despite his apparent concern for you."

"Oh, he is concerned! He has been demanding my hand from father since Angus died, hoping to unite our lands. Apart from my betrothal to Patrick Crawford, that would be the end of the Macdonald clan!"

Blanche did not reply, for she was thinking about this man to whom Fiona had been betrothed as a child, but whom she had never seen. Patrick was the youngest of four sons of a Border chieftain, a few years older than Fiona, and had her father not died the marriage would soon have taken place.

"He is a widower with three young sons, and if I were to marry him no son of mine would inherit my lands," Fiona was saying, almost to herself. "He would make sure his sons took all."

"Have you not sent for Patrick?"

"Yes, but it will take time for him to travel here, and we could not celebrate a marriage for some months. I will be happier and feel safer when he is here, nonetheless: the Campbell frightens me."

It was rare for the self-possessed Fiona to confess to fear, and Blanche set herself to banish as much as she could, talking soothingly until Fiona, worn out with the efforts of the past few days, slept.

The funeral service was long and sombrely splendid, taking place in the small church which served the whole town. Afterwards the funeral procession wound through the narrow streets, lined with keening women who accompanied Lord Hugh, their much loved chieftain, to his final resting place in the vault where most of his ancestors from the past four hundred years lay. By now Blanche was accustomed to the wild cry of the bagpipes, and thrilled when they played gay marching songs and reels. Now she found that in sadness their music pulled forth her own distress and in the fusion the pain was lessened.

The guests, having been solemn for so long, seemed determined to make up for it at the feast which followed. Normally

Fiona would have remained in seclusion, but her position as chieftain forced her to be present, and she endured stoically the sight of the feasting and drinking, taking scarcely any nourishment herself. At last she was able to withdraw from the main hall, but she could not entirely escape, for the most important guests, her family and the neighbouring chieftains, considered it their privilege to accompany her to the smaller room behind the hall. At least it was quieter there, she thought, as she sat beside the fire and steeled herself to endure further company.

Duncan Campbell was assiduous in his attentions, fetching wine and hovering over her while she drank.

"Pray call on me if I can assist you," he said softly so that only Fiona could hear. "I well understand that you will be beset with helpful relatives, but they may not have your true interests at heart as I shall."

Katriona, seeing his attempt to secure Fiona's sole attention, bustled forward.

"You bore up well, my dear, and I am proud of you. Would you not prefer to retire now? I am sure everyone would understand and excuse you."

There was nothing Fiona would have liked better than to escape from these people, but she was not going to leave at Katriona's behest.

"I will do my duty, Aunt," she said coolly, and turned to speak to her Uncle Bruce, who had been trying to catch her attention for some minutes. Impervious to the hint, Katriona drew up a stool and stationed herself beside Fiona, who ignored her.

"You are looking well, Uncle Bruce," Fiona said, smiling at him. He was a gentle looking man, who always seemed worried or distracted, and Blanche had felt sorry for him amongst the rest of these predatory, forceful people.

"Thank you, my dear, I am well. But I have not had time to explain and apologise to you for my dear son's absence. He — he is suffering from a fever, and was unable to travel, but he sends his condolences, and hopes to come to visit you soon."

Colin, who had drawn nearer, gave a crack of laughter. "Your son needs a wife to care for him, Bruce," he said. "How is your dear wife? I trust she is better than when I last heard of her?"

Bruce cast him a glance of sheer loathing; and moved away to stand looking out of the window. Fiona frowned, and with an imperious wave of the hand that deterred even Katriona, followed him and stood chatting quietly with him for a few minutes. Duncan had also moved away, and Katriona beckoned her husband to her side.

"You had best watch Black Duncan," Blanche heard her say. "He means to marry Fiona if he can, and if he succeeds he ends all chance of our sons inheriting."

"I do not think Fiona favours him," Colin muttered.

"That will be nought to do with it. At least she does not favour Bruce's miserable spawn!"

"She is betrothed, in any event."

"Pah! That can be dealt with. 'Tis a great pity that our own Andrew is not old enough to marry Fiona. Twelve is too young, she could not be persuaded to wait for him. Why is Alex not here? I would have expected him to come, for his intention is to wed her himself if he can contrive it!"

"It seems a little premature to start disposing of Fiona almost before my brother is cold in his grave," Colin said slowly.

"Others will not think so, depend on't!"

Katriona rose and, smiling determinedly, passed round the room to converse with the guests. At last she came up to Fiona.

"I have been wondering what your plans are now," she purred. "You can be certain that we mean to aid you, for the rest of your relatives are not fitted to do so!"

"My betrothed will soon be arriving, Aunt Katriona, so that I need not tear you away from your family. Your children must be longing for your return."

"Patrick is on his way?"

"There has scarce been time for my message to reach him, but he will doubtless come as soon as it does, and when a suitable time has elapsed we shall marry."

"I thought to see Alex here, for I am told he is back in Edinburgh. I am surprised that he cannot tear himself away from his entertainments to pay his last respects to his uncle, who was also his chieftain."

"I doubt if he has yet heard. If he had, I cannot imagine any entertainments would keep him away!"

"Some trollop, no doubt!" Katriona said tartly. "You must not permit yourself to be swayed by his charm of manner, my dear. You have had little experience, and I would guide you."

"I know whom to trust," Fiona said sweetly, and politely moved on to talk with someone else.

She was not so calm when she came later that night to Blanche's room.

"That woman! One day I shall be intolerably rude to her! If she does not take herself home within a day or so I shall ask John to abduct her, or spirit her away!"

Blanche laughed, and after a moment Fiona joined in.

"Oh, I should not allow her to disturb me so! But I abhor her managing ways and detestable hints. She is so unkind to poor Uncle Bruce!"

"Why was he so disturbed when she mentioned his wife?"

"Because she has been mad for over ten years, and has to be kept confined. He is terrified that his son, Donald, takes after his mother. I have heard rumours and I think it likely, but so far the poor young man is not seriously enough affected to have to be shut away."

"Poor man! But your other cousin Alexander does not sound so unfortunate."

"No, indeed! Alex is the best of all my cousins, and I believe she is jealous of him, which leads her to disparage him. I do wish that he could have been here. I wonder if he has really returned to Edinburgh?"

On the following day some of the guests departed. Duncan, having contrived to speak alone with Fiona, had been fervent in his assurances that he was anxious only to help her.

"I do understand the sorrow that comes when death removes those we love," he said in a more than usually gentle fashion. "I have lost one very dear to me, and though it is some years ago I still keenly miss her. As do my sons, who are anxious that I should give them a new mother."

"Stepmothers are reputedly hostile to the children," Fiona said lightly, and Duncan laughed.

"Not all. But remember, dear child, rely on me if you need any support. Our people have had much in common despite the enmity that has existed at times. I would end the disputes and have Campbells and Macdonalds live in peace — soon!"

"I could scarce stop shivering," Fiona told Blanche later when she related this conversation. "But now, thank heaven, he is gone and all the others too! I feel charitable towards young Andrew, who is an obnoxious boy, for developing a fever and causing his mother to hasten home!"

Blanche saw less of Fiona in the next few weeks because the affairs of her inheritance occupied her a great deal, but always Fiona enjoyed her leisure hours in the company of Lady Emrey and Blanche, and when he could make time from his duties John often joined them.

Her perceptions keener now that she was older, Blanche had realised as her mother had done long ago that John was devoted to Fiona. He would never hear a word of criticism of her, and served her as steward in a manner that took no heed of anything but her wellbeing. Sometimes Blanche worried over the outcome, and once confided in her mother.

"He must realise that he can never marry her," she said slowly. "Fiona must marry where her father planned."

Lady Emrey smiled down at her and

gently stroked her curls. Blanche was seated on a cushion at her feet, supposedly sewing, but her needle had been discarded long since.

"Do not be concerned over John. I do not believe he wishes for any greater satisfaction than serving his lady, rather in the manner of the knights of chivalry. Odd, mayhap, but in his way he is content. If he loves her, it is not a carnal love. I am sure that some day John will find a woman who stirs his desires in a way Fiona cannot, because he does not allow himself to think of her that way. He will be happy. It will be easier when Patrick arrives."

Blanche was not convinced, for she knew that John never looked at another woman. She could only pray that it would be as her mother thought.

3

THE days passed uneventfully until towards the end of August when Bruce Maclean came on another visit. Fiona received him warmly, for she had always been sorry for this unfortunate uncle who seemed so little fitted to bear his sorrows. They dined together, and afterwards Bruce nervously asked if he might speak alone with Fiona.

"What is it, Uncle?" she asked when he had been comfortably installed in a chair in her private sitting room.

"I am deeply concerned about you, my dear niece," he said, nervously fingering the straggling ends of his moustache. "Have you heard from Patrick? He has not joined this mad venture into England to rescue the King, I trust? Hamilton has no chance of success, none at all!"

"As to that, I cannot tell, but Patrick is not involved. There was a letter a few days ago to say that as soon as he could complete various matters at home he would set out and expected to reach us a week or so after his messenger."

"Then he must be on his way?"

"Almost here, I expect," Fiona agreed, trying to suppress the qualms that were assailing her at the expected advent of this unknown man to whom she was betrothed.

"Reconsider it!" Bruce said suddenly, urgently.

"I beg your pardon?" Fiona was astonished.

"You should not wed him!" her uncle said, twisting his moustache more violently.

"Why ever not?"

"It was not so great a matter before, when your dear brother was alive and would have inherited from your father. Then it was not so important whom you married, though I always considered Hugh was unduly modest in seeking so obscure a match for you. A fourth son, indeed, and a Borderer! No prospects, none whatsoever! What could he have been thinking of?"

Astonished at this outburst from her normally mild uncle, Fiona eyed him with concern.

"Patrick's family are not barbarians,

Uncle," she replied with an uncertain laugh.

"No, no, of course I did not mean that. Of course not. An estimable young man, I am certain, but obscure! You need to marry more in keeping with your status, my dear; an eldest son, one with land to come, one to whom you would be an equal, whose lands might be joined to yours to increase the importance of both! That is necessary in these days, I do assure you, my dear niece. Power can be obtained by judicious marriage alliances."

Fiona was beginning to sense the drift of his words.

"I have no wish to increase my powers," she said sharply. "I consider it my duty to follow my father's wishes in the matter of my marriage, and there is no more to be said, though I do appreciate your concern for my welfare."

"No, not at all. That is, do not your mother's wishes enter into it at all?"

"What do you mean?" she asked, surprised.

He rose from his chair and prowled round the room before answering.

"Your dear mother, my sister, would

have had it otherwise," he said at last. "She was an excellent wife and would never have gone against your dear father's wishes in anything, naturally, but she did confide in me, during her last illness, when she knew that there was no hope of recovery, that she would have liked something else for you."

"Indeed? Pray what was that?" Fiona asked, deceptively calm.

Bruce smiled ingratiatingly. "It is something I myself would like above all things," he said. "That is, for you and my own dear son to unite our two estates. My Maclean lands together with your Macdonald ones would be more than a match for Black Duncan, who menaces us both!"

"So! And what has my cousin to say to this plan? I wonder that he did not come himself to attempt to persuade me!"

"He would have done, was indeed most eager to do so, but he had a most unfortunate hunting accident, and cannot ride for a few weeks. But he wishes it most ardently, I do assure you. He has sent this letter to tell you how greatly he admires you and wishes for the union."

"A most distressing accident! And unfortunate that it cannot be, since I am already promised to Patrick and have no desire or intention of breaking that promise!"

"Oh, come, niece, what harm would there be? 'Tis not as though he comes from a powerful clan close by us, with whom it might cause ill feeling and possibly war!"

"That is not the only reason for keeping faith!" Fiona said sharply.

"Your mother, your dear mother, wished for it!" Bruce said anxiously.

"I hate to have to say, Uncle, that I do not believe you. My mother could not have wished me to marry your son, for she knew even then that he was ill!"

"Oh, you have been misinformed, my dear, absolutely. Donald is a fine young man. Are you worried by that rumour that was circulated, most maliciously, last year, that he was incapable of fathering a child? Naturally we must both be anxious to secure the joint succession to our lands, but the rumour is without foundation! Why, there's a fine healthy babe he fathered on one of the laundry maids to prove it! H'm.

56

Yes, well. You may take my word for it, my dear, there's nought the matter with Donald apart from a slight injury caused by his recent fall!"

Torn between disgust, laughter, and a feeling of pity for the anxious man, so feebly attempting to plead his son's suit, Fiona made it clear that she had no intention whatever of marrying anyone but Patrick, and despondently Bruce departed, his mission a failure.

"I think badly of him for it," Fiona commented when she repeated the conversation to Blanche. "Whatever his misfortunes, he should not have tried to persuade me that my mother would for a moment have countenanced such a match. She knew of his wife's derangement, and often said that Donald's behaviour was reminiscent of his mother's before she succumbed to her malady." She shuddered. "It is appalling for me even to think of such a plan."

The episode was soon forgotten, however, swept away by what happened that evening.

They were at supper when there was a commotion outside, and the great doors of the hall were flung open with a flourish.

Blanche turned and saw a blond giant of a man, well over six feet tall, enter the hall, tossing his cloak to a servant as he strode into the centre of the huge room. For a moment she thought it might be Patrick, but as she saw the nods of greeting he threw to various people she knew that it could not be. John, beside her, had started to his feet at the disturbance, but Fiona quickly laid her hand on his arm and he subsided.

"Cousin Alexander," she said softly, a smile on her lips, "Making his presence known, as usual."

John nodded, recalling the man he had met with Montrose's army. He looked doubtfully at Fiona, who was still smiling in welcome at the tall handsome man striding down the hall towards her, laughingly acknowledging the delighted welcome accorded him by the members of the household.

Alexander reached the table at the end of the hall, where Fiona sat alone except for the Emreys. He surveyed them quickly before bending over his cousin.

"My dearest Fiona — no longer the little cousin I left playing with her dolls," he said caressingly, and pulled her to her feet to kiss her full on the lips as he folded her into a warm embrace.

When she was able to speak, Fiona laughed up at him, her cheeks flushed.

"Alex! 'Tis an age since I saw you. Sit down and tell us all your news."

She made room beside her and he pulled up a stool, looking enquiringly at her companions, and nodding at John in recognition.

"We have not met, or I would have recalled it, Ma'am," he said easily as his glance passed to Lady Emrey and then, lingering for a slightly longer time, to Blanche.

"Lady Emrey, my dear friend," Fiona hastened to introduce them. "Mistress Blanche, who has been my companion these last three years, and Sir John, who was my father's and now is my loyal steward."

Alexander had smiled engagingly at the ladies as Fiona made the introductions, but at these last words he shot his cousin a swift glance, and his eyebrows were raised interrogatively as he turned back to John.

"Steward?" he repeated slowly in a tone of query. "I am certain, Sir John, that you are most loyal!"

John's eyes narrowed, for there was a hint of mockery in Alexander's voice, but before he could answer Fiona spoke again.

"Sir John was a good friend to my brother, and was with him when he died," she explained. "Later my father offered him the post since with the defeat of King Charles, England held no more for him."

"Whereas, I can see, Scotland holds much."

Again there was the slightly mocking tone which turned the words into an insult, John thought angrily. But there was nothing he could reasonably object to, for the words were innocent enough, so he sat without replying while Alexander, his mood becoming grave, told them of the utter defeat of the Scottish army at Preston.

"We got so short a distance, but the rascally English would not venture to join us!" he said scornfully. "The army was crushed like a snail under a man's boot! I doubt if a hundred won free. We were pursued all the way back. I escaped only because I stole a boat and reached the Isles, and from there came back to the mainland. But enough of failure, tell me what has been happening here? You know how distressed I was to be unable to come to Uncle Hugh's funeral. I heard of his death in Edinburgh, but was about to join the Duke of Hamilton, and that could not wait. You do understand?"

Fiona reassured him, then gave him the news, laughingly regaling him with the ludicrous story of her Uncle Bruce's visit to offer her his son's hand.

"His wife is not the only one in the family that wants wit," he remarked. "But Bruce is right in one thing, my love. This marriage with Patrick is no longer wise. You cannot mean to go on with it?"

"I see no reason why not," Fiona replied coldly.

"There are many! You ought to take the opportunity of making a match with a Highland clan."

"And lose the independence we Macdonalds have struggled to maintain? No, Alex, that would be to betray my father."

"Patrick, from all I have heard of him, is no warrior. You need a strong man, Fiona, to help you rule your lands and protect them. No woman is capable of that. You must marry a man capable of fighting for you."

"No doubt you refer to yourself?" she demanded cuttingly.

He grinned at her. "Would you not prefer that? We have the same grandfather: we are both Macdonalds and proud of it. I would fight for you more fiercely and more effectively than any Lowlander!"

Fiona laughed. "You would fight for yourself, I am aware! You do not understand me, Alex! I am the chieftain, and I intend to rule. I, not my husband! You could not suffer any woman who was not subject to you in all things."

He grinned, nodding cheerfully. It seemed to the Emreys that he had completely forgotten their presence, but at that moment he glanced round and briefly his eyes rested on Blanche.

"A woman I loved could rule me in many ways," he said musingly. "So long as she did not make it obvious that she did so. Remember that, my dear!"

"Alex, you are incorrigible!" Fiona exclaimed, and he nodded, unrepentant. "When I marry I will be subject to my husband in all things that are proper, but he shall not rule in my stead! You could not abide that, so let there be no more of this nonsense."

"Then I will sing to you some new songs that I learned in France!"

He sprang up and demanded a lute, and began singing in a deep, attractive voice. The tunes were lively, and when he switched to Scottish ballads most of the people in the hall were singing with him. When the trestles had been cleared away Alexander sprang up with a demand that someone else play, for he had a mind to dance.

Fiona protested that it was unseemly for her to dance so soon after her father's death, though she would have no objection to watching the others, but he swept aside her protests by saying that her father would not have wished to see her moping, denying herself ordinary pleasures. She allowed him to lead her out, ordering the men who had taken his place as musicians to play a reel, and others followed them. John, who had been very silent, partnered Blanche, but she was aware that he watched Fiona all the time, noting her delight in her cousin's return.

At the end of the dance John led Blanche back to where Fiona stood with Alexander. They had almost reached the cousins when Alexander's voice, raised in anger, caused John to halt suddenly and catch Blanche's arm to prevent her from going forward.

"Things have indeed changed, if you can invite your steward to share your table!" he was saying scornfully. "Your father would never have permitted it! It is not seemly to entertain any but the most illustrious guests at your table."

Fiona's reply was inaudible to John and Blanche, but they saw Alexander smile down at her and shake his head.

"Whatever precedent our royal family set, so long ago, we do not have to follow it. I have no doubt that you are lonely, but you must not allow this fellow to impose on you, my dear."

Angrily John stepped forward and Fiona, suddenly aware of him, held out her hands to the two men whose naked hostility flared almost tangibly in the atmosphere.

"I could not fail to overhear your words, my lord," John said through clenched teeth, but Fiona interrupted.

"Alex does not understand!" She turned to him, speaking calmly and evenly. "Father began the custom of having our friends, the Emreys, sit at our table, but whether it was his innovation or mine you have no right to question it! I am the chieftain! Sir John and his family are owed much by us. He spent the last three years of Angus' life fighting beside him, and they were comrades, and his mother tended Angus when he died. Now John serves me and I will not permit you to insult him."

Alexander stared down at her, a quizzical look in his eyes, but she bore his regard steadily, and he suddenly laughed and turned to John.

"I did not intend those words to be heard by you," he said smoothly. "I knew from Angus' letters that you were his friend, and meant no insult. I feel — a degree of responsibility for my cousin, a woman with no man to protect her. Will you accept the apology of a boorish soldier too long absent from polite society?"

He held out his hand and John, his

anger lessened, though he still resented the words, slowly raised his own to grasp it. Alexander grinned engagingly and turned to Blanche.

"Am I also forgiven by you? Will you dance with me while your brother commiserates with my cousin for her deplorable family?"

He did not wait for an answer, but seized her hand and led her into the energetic reel that was about to begin, and she was laughing and dizzy as he whirled her about the room, finally lifting her high above him and spinning round with her at the wild conclusion of the dance.

As he set her down she grasped his arm to steady herself, and with a laugh he immediately slipped his arm about her waist and guided her to a settle near one of the huge hearths.

"Are you exhausted?" he asked, sitting beside her.

"Only for the moment," she replied, tremblingly conscious that he still had his arm round her. "I wonder that you have sufficient energy for this after riding all day."

"I am not finished yet, by all means,"

he warned. "I want to take part in a sword dance later."

He seemed content to sit and talk, however, and so adroit was he in questioning her, and so amusing were his comments, that she almost forgot his arm, left so negligently encircling her waist, until he suddenly hugged her and pulled her to her feet, saying that they had rested long enough and she should dance again.

That was the last dance, apart from the sword dance which Alexander, seemingly tireless, demanded. He and some of the clansmen gave a most intricate, fascinating display, their feet moving so rapidly between and so perilously close to the sharp swords that Blanche held her breath in fear that they would be injured.

At last she went wearily to bed, but she slept so badly that on the following morning there were dark rings round her eyes. Lady Emrey surveyed her in concern.

"You need some fresh air, Blanche," she observed. "I was intending to take this bundle of old clothes to Morag, but as I have many other things to do you can go in my stead."

Blanche gladly agreed. Soon after they had come to Scotland her mother had begun to tend the castle servants and the old retainers, as well as many of the townsfolk, in the same way as she had helped their tenants at home. Lord Hugh had encouraged it, saying that his people had lacked such attentions since his wife had died, and in this way both Lady Emrey and her daughter had become well known, and always welcome when they visited the houses in the town.

Morag had been one of Lord Hugh's nurserymaids, and had been held in especial affection by the whole family, but now she was over seventy years old, a great age, and had for many years been a widow. Lady Emrey always made certain that well before the onset of winter she had plenty of warm clothing, and the bundle she had prepared contained shawls and knitted stockings. Blanche took it and set off for the town, for since her marriage Morag had lived in a tiny house just inside the main town gate. She passed through the castle gateway and then down a flight of steep steps. Below them she had to follow several narrow alleyways, all sloping away from the castle, until she came to the lower town. This was flat, but far less fascinating to Blanche than the twisting lanes huddled close to the castle walls.

While crossing the market place, Blanche stopped to inspect some of the stalls, for the wares displayed never ceased to please her. She was examining a belt of worked leather, marvelling at the intricate workmanship, when a voice behind her said:

"I will take the belt for the lady, Stephen."

Blanche whirled round to see Alexander smiling down at her. He grinned at her startled expression, and took her bundle from her nerveless grasp. Holding her firmly by the elbow, he nodded at the stallholder who was bowing in ecstasy at the large coin that had been given him, and led her away.

"A fine piece of work, is it not?"

Blanche recovered her wits. "I must not accept gifts from you, my lord," she exclaimed, holding out the belt to him.

"Why ever not?"

"It — it is not right," she said, blushing at his amused regard.

"I mean it as a gesture of repentance for

my rudeness yesterday, so surely you will not reject it? If you do, I shall think I am still not forgiven. Besides, I cannot believe that so small a span will encircle your waist," he added calmly, "for 'tis no larger than I could compass with my hands!"

Somewhat flustered, Blanche still tried to protest, but he shook his head and tucked her hand in his arm.

"I meant no insult last night, I do assure you. I was startled, for when I was here before it was certainly no custom for any but the family to sit at that table. I did not realise my uncle had changed it, and as I know that Fiona must be very lonely I thought at first that she was being imposed on. Am I forgiven? Can we not be friends?"

Blanche could not continue to be cold, and he so skilfully put her at her ease that he soon had her talking animatedly, telling him all about her home in England. He was welcomed effusively by Morag, who was full of reminiscences about his escapades as a lad, and after they left the old woman he suggested that if Blanche were not too tired, they walked back to the castle around the top of the ramparts. She readily agreed, for although the walls of the town were not nearly so high as the castle, and somewhat battered in places, one could still obtain an excellent view from them of the surrounding countryside. By the time they returned to the castle Blanche was completely in charity with Alexander, finding him delightful and stimulating company. It was only after she had left him and gone to her mother's apartments that she thought of a reason for his efforts to charm her.

John was there, pacing restlessly up and down while Lady Emrey sat calmly sewing. When Blanche said that she had met Alexander in the town John swung round to her in a fury.

"And no doubt he has bewitched you too! Even his insults last night do not seem to have disgusted you! Do you not realise that he hopes to win us all to his side, knowing that we might be expected to have some influence with Fiona? He is determined to wed her, and wants our support! How thankful I shall be when Patrick Crawford arrives!"

Soon afterwards he left, and Blanche spent the rest of the day gloomily wondering if he were right, and Alexander had sought her company only to ingratiate himself with Fiona's friend.

Fiona herself was preoccupied, for she had many letters to answer, and she wanted to dispose of as many as possible before Patrick arrived, and he was expected at any time.

Restless, Blanche could not settle to anything, and an hour before supper decided to go and see how her horse was. The mare had injured her foot a few days earlier and it was being rested. Blanche wanted to ride out the following day, thinking that it would cure her feeling of disquiet, but if the mare were not fit she would have to make arrangements to borrow one of the other horses. She was crossing the great courtyard on her way to the stables when she noticed a slight commotion as two men came through the gates. One of the men was a carpenter from the town who sometimes did jobs at the castle, and Blanche knew him well. He was supporting the other man, who stumbled along wearily.

"Who is it?" she asked, running towards them.

"I know not, Mistress Blanche. He was found just outside the little east postern gate an hour since, almost senseless. After a drink, all he could say was that he must see the chieftain, and he kept repeating that. I brought him here in my cart."

"Good man. Bring him into the hall, and I will fetch the Lady Fiona."

Calling to some of the men lounging about in this idle hour before supper to give assistance, she sped away to where she knew that she would find Fiona, and told her of the stranger's arrival. Immediately Fiona laid down the quill she was using, tied up a bundle of papers with a leather thong, and then ran down to the hall with Blanche.

The man had been laid on some straw piled into a rough couch before one of the fires, and he was drinking from a tankard. Seeing Fiona he attempted to rise, but she swiftly bent to push him gently back.

"You need rest. Are you badly hurt?" she asked.

"Merely bruised, there are no bones broke, my lady. And I was exhausted, but your good wine has restored me."

"What brings you here in such a

73

condition? Were you set upon by thieves?"

He shook his head and raised his hand to cover his eyes as though to blot out a terrible vision.

"Not thieves, my lady," he whispered at last. "I scarce know how to tell you."

"But you must," Fiona said firmly. "If there is need for action, I can take it only after hearing your story."

Again he shook his head. "I doubt if you can do aught. I — I was travelling with Patrick Crawford. We were crossing the river further south when we were set upon by the rascally boatmen, and others who came out of hiding to assist them. They left me for dead, and I was able to come here to tell you."

Fiona paled. Alexander had entered the hall and was standing behind her, listening to the man intently. He knelt beside Fiona as she crouched beside the man and put a steadying arm about her.

"What happened?" Fiona demanded, refusing to give in to her fears.

"All dead. Every one of us apart from myself."

4

ALEXANDER had led Fiona away after the horrifying news, and had given her into the care of Janet and Lady Emrey. Then he had given orders that the man should be taken to a room near his own, and allowed to rest when his bruises and cuts had been attended to. Supper that night was a very different affair to the gay revelry that had reigned for Alexander's homecoming the night before. Lady Emrey had remained with Fiona, who had been given a posset to make her sleep, and Blanche sat silently while John and Alexander observed an uneasy truce, speculating on who could have been responsible for the deed.

"We shall know better when we hear his full story," John had said at last.

"Thank heaven he is alive to tell it," Alexander had agreed quietly.

It was not until two days later, however, that the man had recovered sufficiently from his ordeal to tell them his story.

Fiona asked Blanche to accompany her to the room where the man lay in bed, propped up on a bank of pillows. Alexander was already there, and John entered soon afterwards.

"Please tell us all you can, and all you suspect," Fiona said softly.

The man nodded, much more alert than he had been when he arrived at the castle, and obviously refreshed by the rest he had had.

"We had travelled up through Glasgow, my lady. My master was cautious and wished to avoid Campbell territory, and so we travelled well past the point where the two rivers meet, intending to cross further down into Maclean lands and work our way back towards you on this bank. It added greatly to the length of the journey, but we thought it would be safer."

Seeing that Blanche looked puzzled, John quickly explained that the Campbell lands referred to lay on the land in between the two rivers, with Glasgow and the Lowlands to the south, and both Maclean and Macdonald lands to the north.

"We found a boat waiting for us, but the messenger we had sent ahead to arrange it was not there. We were told that he had crossed the river earlier to find fresh horses for us, for we had to leave the ones we had, the boat was not able to carry them across. Suspecting no treachery we embarked, and were half way across the river when another boatload of ruffians appeared from cover and came after us. Our boatmen upset the boat, deliberately, I have no doubt, and while we were struggling in the water they attacked us with clubs and stones, while our swords and firearms were of no use to us."

"The cunning devils, whoever they were," Alexander breathed softly.

"Aye," the man agreed. "Methinks they wished it to seem an accident. I heard one of them saying that the bodies would be swept over the weir, and any injuries would be explained by the boat having capsized nearby. The current was strong just there, and that might have been assumed, had I not been fortunate and escaped."

"How did you contrive that?"

"I have always been a strong swimmer, and so I was able to get out of reach of their clubs before they could do me much harm. When I realised what they were about I feigned that I was dead, and floated downstream. I was able to make my way to the bank under cover of some reeds, and I climbed out and hid until they had finished their grisly work. When they had all gone and it was safe to leave, I walked here," he finished simply.

"Did you see Patrick Crawford dead?" Fiona asked. "Can you be certain?"

"Yes, I fear so. He was attacked before the boat was upset, and with a knife that dealt some vicious wounds," the man answered steadily. "Even had he escaped them in the water, which would have been unlikely, for he was a poor swimmer, he could not have survived those wounds. I do so much regret being the one to bring you such sad tidings, my lady."

"It is fortunate for you that you escaped," she returned, "and that you lived to tell the truth of what was done. They shall not escape punishment, whoever they are!"

"Were there any signs by which the men might be identified?" John asked, knowing that it was most unlikely. The man shook his head.

"I have been trying to think and recall every detail," he replied despondently.

"They came from where we took our boat, to the south, and as I was lying hidden I saw them return there afterwards. They dispersed then, and all I could see was that most of them turned westwards, following the river towards the sea."

"What did they wear?"

"Many of them wore plaids of green and blue, but I could not distinguish the pattern, it happened so swiftly, and after I escaped they were too far distant."

"Campbell colours, and they turn towards Campbell lands," Alexander pointed out swiftly.

"It could have been a feint," John pointed out slowly.

"Why should they bother when they were under the impression that all were dead?"

"They might think to have been observed by others," the wounded man suggested. "I could see the smoke from a cottage not far off on the southern bank, though I could not see the place itself, it was hidden by trees."

"Enough, you must rest now." Fiona smiled at him and rose, indicating to the others that she wished them to follow her.

She led the way to her sitting room and looked round at them thoughtfully.

"I wonder who could have been responsible?" she asked.

"Someone who wants to prevent your marriage, obviously," Alexander said. "That could be someone who intends you to have another bridegroom. Black Duncan is the most probable culprit, but it could also have been Bruce Maclean, hoping that you would accept his crazy son."

"Surely not!" Fiona was startled. "Duncan Campbell I could well imagine plotting such murders, but never Uncle Bruce. Apart from all else, he is far too timid!"

"I sometimes wonder if there is a streak of madness in him too, that might make him capable of murder if the rewards are high enough."

They discussed it at length, but could reach no satisfactory conclusion. Fiona, too distressed to concentrate on work, eventually dismissed the men and sat talking quietly with Blanche.

"Alex is right when he says someone wants to prevent my marriage, so it points to Duncan," she said slowly. "He did not seem to realise that after what he has

80

been saying about marrying me himself he might just as easily be suspected on that score!"

"Oh, no!" Blanche exclaimed without thinking. Then she realised that in fact she knew very little of Fiona's cousin, and had not herself been certain whether to trust him or not. "You do not think so, do you?"

Fiona shook her head. "No, for Alex could not have killed them all," she replied calmly. "He is no butcher, and while I believe him capable of killing a man in cold blood as well as in battle, he would not do so wantonly. It is much more believable of Black Duncan!"

"What will you do?"

"What can I do without proof except be on my guard against everyone? But it undoubtedly complicates matters now that I have no prospective husband!"

Blanche looked at her with curiosity. Did she feel no loss for the young man? Fiona read her thoughts and laughed a little bitterly.

"Do not think me heartless, Blanche. After all, I have never met Patrick Crawford, and can have no personal feelings about him.

Naturally I regret his death and the loss it will be to his family, particularly as it was connected with me, but it would have been a political marriage such as I have always known I must make. As my father's heir I cannot marry for love as you will do!"

"I?" Blanche was startled. "I have no thoughts of marriage, Fiona!"

"You should have, you are past seventeen, and many of our visitors have noticed you! John is neglecting his duty towards you; he must find you a husband. Is there anyone you favour?"

Vehemently Blanche shook her head, and Fiona laughed slightly.

"Are you certain? If there is anyone I will do all I can to help you. I think John would listen to me if I expressed my wishes on such a matter."

"No!" Blanche was firm in her denial, finding the very thought of marriage distasteful after this evidence of the passions and jealousies it could arouse.

Fiona smiled. "We must both seek for husbands, then," she said lightly. "I have just three years, think you that will be long enough?"

"Why so?"

"My father had rather strange ideas. He had no doubts about my fitness to succeed him, but he was convinced that a woman needed a husband, and more especially if she ruled great estates. There was an odd provision in his will which stipulated that if I were not married by my twenty-first birthday, his lands, and the chieftainship, would pass to Colin or the next male heir. Of course he did not imagine that he would not himself still be alive, or that Patrick would die, but you can see that it complicates matters."

"Does your uncle know of this?" Blanche demanded.

"Oh yes."

"Then — if he could prevent your marriage — "

"Exactly. He would gain the chieftainship he has always wanted."

"So it might have been Colin instead of Bruce or Duncan?"

"It could have been, although I do not think he would have the resolution!"

"His wife would," Blanche declared. "Does Alexander know of this clause?"

"I imagine not, or he would have denounced Colin along with the others.

I cannot decide whether to tell him yet. I do not wish him to begin hurling accusations at our uncle while we have no kind of proof."

"But he ought to be warned!"

"Warned?"

"He will be in danger," Blanche said worriedly.

"How is that?"

"If he becomes betrothed to you!"

Fiona stared at her and then laughed, the first genuine amusement she had shown for some time.

"Blanche, my dearest friend, are you mad too? I could never, never marry Alex! Oh, he is charming, and I like him, and enjoy his company, but he would make me a dreadful husband, for we would always be quarrelling! He is overbearing at times, and would most decidedly think it his right to rule, and it is not! I will take no man to husband who does not understand that. I do not mean to be a domineering wife, but my chieftainship is a position of sacred trust. Do you understand?"

"Yes, of course. Poor Fiona! You are unfortunate in having this consideration in choosing a husband."

"It is my destiny, but you are a great comfort to me, Blanche. Enough of this now. I have no doubt that as soon as Patrick's death becomes common knowledge my relations will descend on me to offer their false condolences. Let us go riding and forget them while we may!"

Fiona was correct in her expectation that her relatives would soon appear. Both her uncles arrived on the following day and insisted on staying for some time, much to Fiona's chagrin. The only satisfaction was that Katriona had been prevented from coming by the sudden illness of one of her children.

"Thank goodness for children and their ailments!" Fiona commented when she and Blanche had contrived to slip away from the castle for a few hours. "Uncle Colin is bad enough on his own, but it is far more than twice as bad when they are both here!"

At last the uncles departed, Colin attempting to make Fiona promise to go and stay with him and his family for a while. She made excuses, saying what a great amount of work she had to do, and instantly regretted it when he seemed to reconsider his departure, saying that he felt it his duty to remain and help her with it.

"No indeed, Uncle. Aunt Katriona is expecting you home, and will be anxious for your company and support if the children are worse!"

"Yes, my dear, so thoughtful of you to remember that. Oh, my goodness, in all the excitement I nearly forgot. Your aunt sent you this little gift of sweetmeats, for she remembers what a sweet tooth you have. Now be sure to take good care of yourself."

"Indeed I will," Fiona assured him.

No sooner had Colin and Bruce departed than Fiona received a visitor from the Campbells. In considerable state a cavalcade of horses wound its way up the hill and into the castle courtyard. With immense dignity a superbly attired personage dismounted from the most magnificently caparisoned horse, and consented to enter the castle. Fiona, hastily informed of the arrival, came down to give him welcome, and they retired into her sitting room with another of the visitors, remaining closeted together for several hours.

86

"Who is it?" Blanche asked Alexander when he, having returned from hunting, came to seek her out and discover how long the visitors had been here.

"An embassy from Duncan," he replied tersely. "No doubt he brings false commiserations on Patrick's death! That devil attempting to overawe us with ostentation by bringing a more important Campbell chieftain to his aid."

"But it would not take so long, surely, to present such a message."

"So there must be something else, and I'll hazard I know!"

He said no more, but strode off to pace restlessly up and down the gallery from which Fiona's sitting room opened. It was almost supper time before Fiona emerged, and though Alexander started forward to speak with her she gave him no opportunity of saying what he intended.

"Ah, Alex, you recall Lord Iain? He has been kind enough to bring me messages from Duncan Campbell. I rely on you to assist me in entertaining him properly."

She smiled and turned to Lord Iain, leading him away along the gallery and chatting of inconsequential matters, while Alexander, for once speechless, stood watching her.

There was no occasion during supper for either Blanche or Alexander to talk with Fiona, for she was fully occupied in entertaining her visitors lavishly. Towards the end of supper she beckoned to John and he approached her chair. After a few words introducing him to Lord Iain, who graciously praised him for the prosperous looks of the estate, Fiona leaned back, her head turned away from Lord Iain, while John bent his head close to hers to catch her whisper.

"I must speak with you when we are all retired. Can we meet in Blanche's room secretly? Ask Alex to be there also."

She raised her voice, glancing back towards Lord Iain. "You will enjoy hearing our pipers, Lord Iain. My steward will arrange it."

John nodded, seeming to have no cares, and Fiona gave all her attention to her guest. John retired and spoke to the pipers, then unobtrusively left the hall. Shortly afterwards Alexander felt a tug on his sleeve, and looked round to see a small page, eager and self-important, stretching up to whisper in his ear.

"The steward wishes to speak with you a moment, my lord, and he said could you come unnoticed?"

"Where is he?"

"Just outside the hall, in the gallery."

Alexander nodded. "Tell him I will be with him in a moment."

He turned to drain his tankard, and then, after a few comments to his neighbour, rose and excused himself. Slipping quietly from the hall he found John half concealed in a window embrasure, and raised quizzical eyebrows at him.

"Well, why the mystery?"

"Lady Fiona wishes to talk with us both in secret. We are to meet in my sister's room when everyone else is abed." Alexander opened his lips and then, deciding to remain silent, closed them grimly, staring at John.

"The chieftain commands," John added softly.

"An odd place of assignation," Alexander sneered, and John flushed angrily.

"You overrate yourself, my lord!" he snapped contemptuously, and Alexander suddenly chuckled.

"Then you had best meet me to direct me, else I could not find my way," he replied silkily.

When the rest of the castle had retired, the four of them congregated in Blanche's room. Fiona began.

"I dare not risk Lord Iain seeing me consult you out of the ordinary way," she said apologetically, "but there are several matters I need advice on."

"I understood you to wish to rule alone," Alexander grinned at her.

"Peace, Alex. I still need advice, though the decision must be mine alone. First, Lord Iain has said that he is proposing to collect an army to march into England and release the King, and wants to know how many fighting men I could spare. He suggested he reviewed them himself tomorrow. Would it be wisest to tell him only a few, to lull Duncan's suspicions, to mislead him?"

"You surely do not suspect him of planning an attack on you?" Blanche asked, horrified.

Fiona laughed bitterly. "I have been given a strong enough warning!"

"Was that all he came for?" Alexander

queried in surprise.

"Not ostensibly. He brought a very flattering offer for my hand, or so he told me! He spared himself no pains to point out that his kinsman could have selected any number of more eligible brides, but his personal feelings entered into this, and he was determined to wed me. He left me in no doubt of that determination, implying that if force would be necessary, force would be used."

"This is monstrous!" John exclaimed.

"Aye, but not unusual in the alliances of Highland clans, where lands and power are at stake, and everyone else is so taken up with their own affairs that they would not object, and most decidedly would not interfere," Alexander informed him.

"That is another question," Fiona continued. "Shall I make my rejection clear, for nothing would ever induce me to wed such a one, or shall I prevaricate? Which would be best?"

"If you give him hope and say you have few men, you will encourage him to attack," Alexander commented.

"A firm refusal might enrage him," John said slowly, "but I agree about the soldiers. Show him a strong force, as strong as we have, and that might give him pause. How many men has he?"

"A band of ruffians," Alexander said caustically. "Unfortunately no-one can be sure of his strength. He has a small troop which he normally keeps with him, but there are also, I hear, bands of men stationed all around his lands. Many of these are hardened soldiers and I strongly suspect one of these groups was responsible for Patrick's murder."

"Then we need to discover more."

"How can we do that?" Fiona asked.

"By sending someone to discover it. 'Tis an idea. I will dye my hair and go myself," Alexander suggested, smiling at the thought of such an adventure.

"No, Alex, that would be folly!" Fiona said sharply. "You are far too well known in all of Scotland."

"With disguise, and if I kept out of the way of the better folk, I would not be recognised," Alexander protested.

"Your height and looks could not be disguised, however you dyed your hair. John, is there anyone suitable to be trusted with such a mission?"

"One or two who might achieve success, but I would prefer to go myself."

"No! You cannot leave us unprotected!" Fiona exclaimed, and Blanche, who had been sitting back quietly, taking no part in the discussion, saw Alexander glance swiftly at his cousin and frown at this show of agitation.

He cannot be jealous of John, she thought in dismay, when there was no possibility of Fiona and John marrying. But Fiona did sound unduly perturbed, so was it at all possible that she loved John? Blanche did not think it likely, but as these thoughts flashed through her mind John was replying.

"Your cousin is a soldier and well able to protect you if he will remain here. He cannot go, I agree, for he would be certain to be recognised. But I am not well known, and with the present situation in England what could be more natural than an Englishman who is travelling through Scotland — on the way to friends?"

"We could send one of the men," Fiona said urgently, but John shook his head.

"Though it is a task another man could

do, I think I would stand more hope of succeeding. This is a matter in which we cannot afford errors."

"I do not like it," Fiona said worriedly.

"But I fear he is possibly right," Alexander said suddenly. "I will remain here, Sir John. If Fiona sends an answer that it is too early for her to be thinking of another husband so soon after Patrick's death — mayhap we had best lull Duncan's suspicions regarding what we suspect of that too — he might consider it better strategy to wait rather than use force. That would give us time to learn more about his strength."

"It is our best ploy," John urged.

"Unless you marry another at once, before Duncan can move," Alexander suggested, laughter in his eyes as Fiona turned angrily towards him.

"And whom do you suggest?" she cried wrathfully. "Young Donald? That imbecile!"

"I could suggest a worthier mate for you," he answered with aggravating calm.

"Yourself, no doubt!"

"Do you then accept me, dear cousin? Somehow I had thought you as averse to me as to poor Duncan!"

"I am indeed! You are quite as ruthless as he in obtaining your wishes regardless of others!"

"You wrong me. I sometimes help others to realise what their true wishes are, those that they conceal out of some misguided notions!"

Fiona turned away from him, breathing deeply, and began to question John about his plans. Alexander sat back watching them in amusement, and when he caught Blanche looking at him, smiled and winked at her. Hastily she looked away, drawing a low chuckle from him.

"Then you will go as soon as Lord Iain has left," Fiona said to John. "I will send a reply as Alex suggested. How long will your preparations take? Shall I contrive to detain Lord Iain?"

"I can leave tomorrow," John assured her. "There is no reason to keep the fellow here for longer than you wish."

Fiona sighed. "I fear he will not go tomorrow, but I will attempt to send him away as soon as possible. His very presence angers me as much as it perturbs me!"

"No need, with me to protect you, and

Sir John busy with his work," Alexander said softly.

Fiona looked at him silently for a moment, then turned apologetically to Blanche.

"I am sorry to have used you and your room so, my dear, but there was nowhere else I could think of where we might converse secretly."

"I wish I could help in some other way," Blanche returned, smiling sympathetically at her friend.

"Just by being with me!"

The following day, while Fiona was again closeted with Lord Iain, Blanche walked on the terrace, admiring the brilliant display of the autumn leaves, and the softer, endless vista of heather and broom-covered moorland stretching away into the distance as far as she could see. The loch twisted away below her around the foot of the castle, and she leaned on the parapet gazing down into the still, deep water and thinking of the undercurrents there had been the previous evening. She was afraid that John might have shown his feelings for Fiona too plainly, which could be dangerous for him if Alexander recognised them. Fiona herself did not appear entirely indifferent to John, but seemed as determined as ever against marriage with her cousin, despite what Blanche thought was his obvious intention on the matter.

"Are you wishing yourself back in England?" a voice close to her ear said, and Blanche whirled round to find that Alexander had approached silently to stand close beside her.

"You startled me, my lord," she exclaimed, taking a step backwards. "No, I have no particular desire to return there, for Scotland now seems like home."

He smiled. "I know that you are my cousin's very dear friend and companion. Will you not be lonely when she weds?"

Blanche looked at him closely, attempting to read the look in his eyes.

"I expect I will," she said at last.

"You must marry then also. Has Fiona a husband in mind for you?"

"Lady Fiona has been most kind," Blanche said a little stiffly.

"You are truly fond of her. You would not wish her to be in danger?"

"Danger?" Blanche stared at him. "In

97

what way is she in danger apart from Duncan Campbell?"

"Not from him alone, though I suspect he is the most urgent danger we have to deal with. There are others who might attempt to force Fiona's hand in the matter of her marriage, or even murder her."

Blanche breathed deeply. "Who is it that you suspect?" she demanded.

Alexander shrugged. "All who stand to gain by her death or marriage. Bruce and Duncan hope to win more land for themselves, so for them marriage is the only way. But Colin would benefit only by her death."

"Surely he would not kill her!" Blanche was horrified.

"He may have killed Patrick," Alexander reminded her. "With that clause in my uncle's will he would gain from killing Patrick only if Fiona remains unwed for three more years, and that I do not expect."

"So you do know about that!"

He raised his eyebrows mockingly. "Would you expect me to neglect to discover all I could about such a matter?" he asked lazily. "I am also in line for the chieftainship, or had you forgot?"

"You are not very close!" Blanche retorted, allowing her annoyance with him to show in her voice.

"True, by birth," he murmured, and she shot an angry glance at him to find him eyeing her in amusement. "Peace, my little one! We both have Fiona's welfare at heart — "

"Do you indeed?" Blanche interrupted, and he laughed.

"Naturally. She is in danger. She recognises this, I think, but if we, her friends, can impress on her the seriousness of it while she delays in choosing a husband, we will be aiding her."

"And just whom do you suggest, her cousin Donald? I assume you would not advocate Duncan's suit!"

"Oh no, and not Donald, either, I think. It would be a stupid waste to give so lovely a bride to a sot incapable of appreciating his good fortune. Do you not think Fiona lovely?" he added unexpectedly.

"Yes, and worthy of a good husband who will protect her!" Blanche snapped.

"I do agree. She is one that is made for love, not for the tedious business of managing an estate."

"But she intends to control her inheritance."

"Unwise. 'Tis no task for a woman."

"I disagree. What of Elizabeth of England? She was a most successful ruler."

"But not a successful woman too. Those Queens that allow love to enter their lives always fail. What of Mary of Scotland, and Mary Tudor?"

Blanche stared at him, unable to think of any other successful women rulers, and he laughed gently.

"It is not the same, the chieftainship," she said weakly. "Many women must have successfully managed estates."

"In any event, if Fiona would remain chieftain she must marry. And a woman must be obedient to her husband, do you not agree, Mistress Blanche?"

"Fiona's position is not the same as that of any other woman, though," Blanche argued.

"I would not envy any husband who accepted that. He would be in an intolerable position himself."

"You would not allow it, I think you mean to say!" Blanche flung at him.

He shook his head, smiling at her, and she fumed.

"As Fiona's friend, pray urge her to hasten in her choice of a husband," he repeated, smiling down at her. "I rely on your friendship."

"To urge your suit, my lord?" Blanche was scornful. "You can scarce expect my good offices when I know your intentions vary so greatly from those of my friend! I will be no traitor to her, of that you can be sure!"

He looked down at her for a long moment in silence, his expression inscrutable, but she could not decide whether he was angry or amused. Somehow the thought of his amusement made Blanche more furious than the thought of his possible anger. She stared back defiantly.

"You know my intentions?" he asked at length, holding her gaze steadily.

"You make them very plain, sir! But there are many other possible alliances for Fiona than any that you have suggested. She does not need to look only to her relations or the Campbells."

"Agreed, but somehow I think that she will find what she needs close by."

Unsmiling, he turned and left her, and Blanche found herself trembling. It was the cold, she hastily assured herself, for the autumn wind could be very chill in the Highlands. Suddenly the forests and mountains before her seemed less friendly than hitherto. The sense of danger, for herself as well as Fiona, was strong at that moment, and with some haste Blanche almost ran along the terrace towards her own apartments.

5

JOHN was busy making his secret preparations to visit the Campbell lands, and Blanche, occupying herself with some embroidery in her room, was surprised when he came to see her.

"Do you need some help?" she asked.

"No, I thank you. All this talk of marriage for Fiona has put me in mind of the plans I was hoping to make for you, before Lord Hugh's death caused me to delay."

Blanche was startled. This was the first time John had indicated that he was making any plans for her.

"What manner of plans?" she asked quickly, her voice a little tight with an emotion she realised was fear.

"Why, marriage, naturally. I ought to have settled the matter years since, but our coming here to Scotland and the completely new life we have led stayed my hand. I will admit that in part I waited in order to see how the King's fortunes changed. I have been corresponding, as you know, with the good rector at home. He tells me of what is done to the Manor, and he writes to tell me that he has found a possible husband for you."

She was surprised. "There was no-one suitable when we lived there. Yet I suppose, since I now have no dowry, what was once suitable is so no longer. Who is it?"

"It is the son of the new owner of the Manor."

"A Parliamentarian?" Blanche exclaimed in horror, staring at her brother wide-eyed.

"As to his politics, all men must outwardly support the King's vanquishers."

"He is one of them!"

John shrugged unhappily. "I realise that. Mr Henderson writes, however, to say that he has spoken of you to them, and the man feels some qualms of remorse for having dispossessed us. He suggested a marriage with his son as a form of recompense. It would bring the Manor back to the family."

Blanche did not reply, and John continued. "I have no wish to overpersuade you. Mr Henderson tells me that he is the elder son, twenty-five years of age, well set up and with a handsome fortune to come from his father in addition to the Emrey lands."

"As ill gotten, no doubt!"

"We cannot tell. He must have some proper feeling, though, to consider you. That is why I have entertained the notion. I would not have done so had he appeared utterly heartless."

"Is he the wretch that turned us out that day?" she asked bitterly.

"No. Mr Henderson stressed that he came only much later. His was not the original outrage."

"But I would have to return to England," Blanche said almost to herself.

"You must have thought that a possibility some day?" John asked.

"Do you ever intend to return?" she responded quickly, and John looked dubious.

"I hoped to be able to take you to England if the King's affairs had prospered," he said evasively. "I have not given much thought to it."

Blanche was silent, attempting to understand her varied emotions. She had realised that a marriage must soon be arranged for her, but her life was so contented that she had been pleased not to know of any plans her mother and brother might make. Now it seemed that she must leave Scotland and Fiona, and the prospect was far from pleasing.

"What is his — this man's name?" she asked at length. "And will I be able to meet him before — before — "

"We shall not force you into any match against your will," John reassured her quickly. "I wrote to our friend asking him if he knew of anyone suitable, and he has been making enquiries. He showed the miniature I had painted of you to this man and his family, and they were interested in the match. I will confess that I have sometimes hoped that you might meet a suitable man here, and then if I do not, or am unable to return to England, we could still be together. There is no-one, I think?"

He considered the young men Blanche knew, friends of the Macdonalds, men from the town, visitors from other clans, and though he was well aware that Blanche received some flattering attention from many of them, she did not appear to have any preference for one more than another.

"There is no-one," Blanche said hurriedly. "What is his name?"

"Roger Grant. If you are agreeable I will write and suggest that the young man journeys here to meet you."

"I would prefer to stay with Fiona," Blance said suddenly. "I do not wish for marriage, and to have to leave you and mother and go back to England!"

"Fiona will soon be married herself, and will become so taken up with her husband and the affairs of her estates that she can do without your company," John said abruptly, a harsh note in his voice. "It would indeed be better for you to leave rather than suffer through any change in her."

"Fiona would never change!" Blanche declared in defence of her friend, but she had a faint suspicion that he might be right; that once Fiona were married her interests would inevitably be separate from those of Blanche.

"Then I will write to Mr Henderson. I must do it before I leave, and 'twill be one less matter of concern."

Lord Iain Campbell left on the following day, and John one day later. He did not speak again with Blanche on the matter of the proposed marriage, and she did not know whether he had written to England. She did not care to discuss the prospect with her mother, feeling that this would indicate her willingness to accept such an arrangement, and determinedly thrust the whole business to the back of her mind.

Fiona was preoccupied with her estates, but always delighted in Blanche's company when she had time to spare. A week went by after John's departure, but there was no message from him. Both Blanche and Fiona knew full well that it was most unlikely that he would be able to entrust a message to anyone, but they both nonetheless hoped to receive some word from him. Life was almost dull with no excitement to break the even flow of the days, only the constant anxiety, until one morning Blanche was awoken early by a hand shaking her urgently.

"What is't?" she asked in alarm, struggling out of a deep sleep. "John? Is it John?"

"No, missee, 'tis my dear mistress. Oh, I beg you, come to her at once!"

Blanche's sleepy eyes focused on the worried face of Janet, Fiona's old nurse, bent close to her own. The candle she held cast weird shadows about the room as she hastily set it down on a table beside the bed and dragged the bed curtains further aside, reaching for Blanche's wrap as she did so.

"What is it? What ails Fiona?" Blanche asked in alarm as she slid out of bed and thrust her feet into the slippers Janet held out to her, and pulled the wrap round her shoulders, shivering at the cold.

"Come, I will explain as we go," Janet whispered, but she led the way so swiftly along the draughty passageways and down a narrow flight of stairs that Blanche had no time to question her, and learned only that Fiona was ill. Reaching Fiona's bedchamber Janet pulled her inside and whispered in her ear.

"Do not ask questions until the physician has gone," she warned.

Blanche was too astonished by the scene that met her gaze to argue. Several candles had been lit, and Fiona lay motionless in the great bed where all the chieftains had lain. At her side the man who was the castle's physician had just finished bleeding her, and was in the act of removing the bowl that held the blood.

"That should remove some of the evil humours," he muttered fussily, then glanced across at Janet. "Give her this potion in an hour, it will complete the purging. I will return soon."

He left the room and Blanche stood looking down at her motionless friend in wide-eyed alarm.

"What happened?" she said softly to Janet as the latter began to bathe Fiona's temples with a cloth soaked in a sweet smelling substance that Blanche could not recognise.

Janet looked up at her, a grim expression in her eyes.

"I did not tell the physician all," she said in a low voice. "He is well enough at his trade, but he is a fool, and I do not entirely trust him. If aught happened to my dear lady, he would repeat my suspicions."

"What suspicions? What ails Fiona?"

"She was poisoned."

"What? But how, when? She was perfectly well when we went to bed last night, for she came to my room and we talked for a while, as we often do."

"I believe 'twas afterwards. My nurseling

always had a sweet tooth and she kept a box of comfits here in her room, and had them when she felt like one. I cannot say whether she had one last night after I had seen her into bed, but the box is beside her bed and she could have taken one. I looked in on her an hour afterwards, for she had seemed restless, and I thought she might want some mulled wine to help her sleep. She was twisting in agony on the floor and could scarce speak. She had vomited and I suspected poison, so I gave her a remedy of my own which caused her to vomit again. Then I fetched the physician and he has been purging and bleeding her since."

"Will she recover?" Blanche demanded fearfully.

"Surely, for she is not so ill as others I have seen that have been poisoned."

"Are you sure it was the comfits? Could it not have been something she ate at supper?"

"It could, but you are not ill, and neither am I nor the physician, nor several other people I have seen," Janet said swiftly. "As soon as it is light I shall go and give the rest to one of the stable dogs."

Blanche stared at her in consternation.

111

"If it is the comfits, then it must have been deliberate," she said slowly. "Where did they come from? The castle kitchens?"

Janet pursed her lips. "No. That is why I do not tell any but you until I am more certain. They were a present from her loving Aunt Katriona, brought here by her Uncle Colin," Janet replied in a flat, expressionless voice.

"And you think — ? No, they would not! Surely they would not dare?"

"They have much at stake," Janet reminded her.

"What will you do?"

"Guard my mistress carefully until she is better, and then tell her, for 'tis her decision whether to accuse them." Janet turned away, starting to clear up the things used by the physician. "I had to tell someone else for fear aught happened to me," she said in a muffled voice, and great sobs began to rack her. "You are her friend, you love her as I do," she gasped.

"Hush, Janet, you have saved her this time, and must not give way," Blanche urged, taking the old woman in her arms and holding her close. "I will help you guard her and look after her, and there will be no further opportunity for them. You know you can trust me. Come now, there is work to do, and we must tidy the room before she sees this confusion!"

Janet gulped and sniffed and patted Blanche's hand.

"I knew you were her friend," she muttered, and nodded several times. "I do not think we ought to tell anyone else until my lady has considered it."

Blanche agreed, for the attempt had been a great shock, and she could not disentangle her whirling thoughts. She wished intensely that John were there, so that she could unburden herself to him, and on the thought she recalled that Alexander, with his promise of guarding Fiona, perhaps ought to be informed. But when she suggested this to Janet some time later the old woman was reluctant.

"Best tell no-one," she insisted. "I am sure Lord Alexander is to be relied on, but the fewer to know the less likely that our suspicions will get abroad, and that will be safer for my mistress, which is all I care about."

"What shall we tell people in the castle?

We must say something to account for the illness."

"A stomach disorder. We cannot hide that, for the physician will talk. But possibly you could pretend to be a little affected and blame the fish we had? You and your mother will have shared the one at my lady's table, and Alexander also. If another is affected it will divert attention from other possible causes."

Blanche nodded eagerly. She appreciated the old woman's desire to hide the real cause of Fiona's illness until there was more proof, or until John returned, and Fiona was well enough to make her own decision on how to deal with the situation.

"I will stay here with Fiona and give it out that I too am indisposed."

"And for fear it was not the comfits, I will prepare all the food for you both," Janet declared fiercely.

They sat watching over Fiona until the dawn spread a faint light over the castle. She had slept heavily, but when the pipes that were always played to herald the sunrise were heard she opened her eyes. Blanche bent over her.

"Oh, my head! Blanche, why are you

here so early?" she asked weakly.

"Hush, you must stay there, you have been ill."

"Ill? What is it? Oh, this detestable taste in my mouth! I must have something sweet!"

She stretched out her arm towards the box in which the comfits had lain, but it was empty. At that moment Janet came up with a glass of wine in her hand.

"Drink this, my dearie, 'tis what you need to strengthen you."

Weakly Fiona complied, and after staring in a puzzled way at Blanche, closed her eyes and drifted back to sleep. For the rest of that day she alternately slept and lay drowsily, too ill to ask questions, but grateful that Blanche remained beside her.

Janet bustled about, giving orders to the maids as to what they were to say, and sending them running to bring food and all the other things she demanded. Janet and Blanche ate bread and cheese, for as the old woman remarked grimly, these could hardly be tampered with.

"I will go and kill a chicken myself, and we will have that later, and it will make a

115

nourishing broth too," she promised, and as soon as she was satisfied that all was in hand she departed, taking what were left of the comfits with her.

While she was gone Lady Emrey came to discover what was the matter, but Blanche met her in the anteroom and explained that Fiona had been ill during the night and wished for her company.

"Janet is in charge," she said with a slight laugh, for now that Fiona seemed to be sleeping calmly she was no longer afraid. "It seems to her as if Fiona is back in the nursery!"

Lady Emrey smiled and nodded. "Your own nurse revelled in any illness that kept you her prisoner for a while," she agreed, and Blanche shivered. "Are you ill too, my dear?" her mother asked anxiously.

"No, 'tis that Janet has made such a large fire in Fiona's room that standing here out of its range I feel cold," she explained, and then recalled that Janet wanted it to be believed that she too was ill. Surely Janet would not expect her to deceive her mother. She explained quickly, begging her mother not to breathe a word of their suspicions to anyone else, and saying that she was going to pretend to be feeling ill also if anyone else came.

"I pray Janet is not right," Lady Emrey said calmly. "Now you had best go back to Fiona, and I will return later to see if I can help Janet."

She left the anteroom, and Blanche returned to her post at Fiona's side. Soon afterwards Alexander appeared in the anteroom and Blanche went swiftly out to him, her finger to her lips.

"Hush, Fiona sleeps," she said urgently.

"I must see her, to make certain she is well."

"She is far from well, so you cannot see her! But Janet says she is in no danger," Blanche told him, standing firmly in the doorway separating the rooms so that he could not pass.

"Do you presume to give me orders?" he asked in surprise, halting before her as she refused to move out of his way.

"I care only that Fiona be not disturbed," she replied calmly, firmly repressing the desire she had to step backwards away from his large and menacing presence.

"I have certain rights here, Mistress

Emrey, and of that you must be aware," he said haughtily.

"Mayhap, but disturbing your chieftain when she is in dire need of sleep is not one of them," snapped Blanche. "Lower your voice, if you please!"

For a moment he stared at her arrogantly, then his expression changed and he grinned engagingly. Blanche had been trembling because of her defiance of him, and now she put out a hand to steady herself against the doorpost.

"I apologise, for I understand that you are indisposed yourself," he said in a milder tone, and surveyed her mockingly so that she blushed in confusion. "I would have said that you were far too vehement in defence of Fiona, and indeed looking delightfully healthy, to be suffering greatly."

"I — I have been much less severely affected than Fiona," Blanche stammered.

"Indeed? I am happy to hear that. But you do appreciate my anxiety about my cousin?"

"We are all anxious, but it is a mere disorder of the stomach, and she sleeps. When Janet returns she will tell you when you may see Fiona."

"So the old dragon is in her element again, is she? Lord, how she used to terrify us as children!"

"And will do so again, so be it that you disturb my lady," Janet's admonishing voice came from behind him.

Alexander swung round to face her. "She will recover?" he demanded.

"To be sure, stupid boy! What a commotion to make over a mite of sickness! Tomorrow you may see her, but not for long, mind! And you must not plague her with problems!"

"No, ma'am!" he replied, but smiled and dropped a kiss on her wrinkled cheek as he passed her. "I'll keep you to your word."

Janet watched him unsmilingly as he left the room, and then gave Blanche a faint smile as she took the chicken she carried into the bedroom.

"Shall you tell him?" Blanche asked, following her and pulling a stool up before the fire. "I will pluck the bird while you prepare the rest."

"I shall tell no-one else," Janet said. "'Tis not that I do not trust young Alex, but the fewer that know the better. Besides,

119

he might do something rash against his uncle."

It was two days before Fiona was able to leave her bed, and she was very weak and easily tired. Janet, who had taken complete charge of her apart from the visits of the physician, gave strict orders that she was only to attempt to sit out in a chair for an hour on the first day, and Fiona was only too pleased to obey, finding herself more feeble than she had ever been before. But the following day she felt much stronger, and commanded Blanche to tell her what had happened. Janet was in the room, and she subjected Fiona to a sharp scrutiny before nodding her head.

"I will lock the outer door," she said, and proceeded to do so, somewhat to Fiona's amazement.

"Are we in some danger?" she asked.

"Possibly. I do not know. Did you, my lady, eat one of the sweetmeats out of your box the night before you were ill?"

Fiona frowned in concentration. "Yes, I think I did. Then afterwards I had a bitter taste in my mouth and felt sick. I tried to get out of bed, but — I remember no more!"

Janet nodded and explained her suspicions. "I gave the rest of them to one of the dogs, but he suffered no ill effects, so none of the others were poisoned."

"It could not have been that then."

"It could have been just one sweetmeat treated with a poison, so that you would eat it at some time. You were fortunate that it caused you to vomit, else it would have killed you."

"But — Aunt Katriona sent those to me!"

"Yes," was all the reply Janet vouchsafed to this.

Fiona eyed her in dismay. "I cannot believe that she would do that!"

"You are too honest and trusting! She is a wicked woman, and I've always said so. She is like a she-wolf where her cubs are concerned. She has those two boys to provide for, and your Uncle Colin is not wealthy. His wife has always resented his being the second son."

"They could have killed Patrick," Blanche said quietly. "I have been puzzling over this, Fiona, and if it was Katriona, it well might have been her plot against Patrick too. She may think that the only safe plan would be to kill you also. To kill your betrothed would not suffice, for you are not likely to remain unwed. She must rid herself of you if she wants Colin to become chieftain."

"Uncle Colin brought me those comfits. I cannot believe he would agree!"

"He is too timid," Blanche agreed, "but he need not have known what he gave you."

"I might have given them to someone else."

"Your aunt knows your habits," Janet reminded her. "Whenever you have stayed with her you have kept some beside your bed. And if by some mischance the poisoned one were to be eaten by someone else, that would be a setback, nothing more. She would try again. It was clever to make only one sweetmeat poisonous, for no proof could then be found in the others."

Janet was so positive in her opinion that Fiona, despite her natural revulsion at the thought of her aunt attempting to murder her, was almost convinced.

"What shall we do?" she asked. "Have you told Alex of these suspicions?"

Janet hesitated, seeming reluctant to

answer. "I think it wisest not to," she said slowly. "I would not wish to alarm your aunt if talk of our suspicions got back to her. As it is, she will not be certain that your illness is caused by the poison, and will hold her hand awhile. Your cousin is so impetuous he would mayhap wish to confront them. I would wait until your steward returns. He will know what to do and can be trusted to do what is best, and not act hastily. In the meantime I am preparing all your food as a precaution, and I sleep in the anteroom with the door locked so that no one can enter. You are safe, my lady."

"I am honoured that you care so well for me," Fiona said, smiling at her old nurse, and Janet pursed her lips.

"You need someone, until you have a good husband," she said gruffly, but obviously proud of the praise.

For another week Fiona kept to her room, gradually recovering her strength, but oddly reluctant to resume her normal life again. John was still absent, and now that her concern over Fiona had lessened, Blanche found herself worrying much of the time about his safety. Fiona seemed indifferent, for when one morning as the two girls sat sewing Blanche expressed these fears, Fiona merely smiled calmly.

"He will return, I have that certainty," she said. "He warned me that he might be gone for several weeks, for to gather exact information he might need to travel over great distances."

"I wish he would return here, so that we can plan what to do about all your enemies," Blanche replied to this. "Have you had any message from your Aunt Katriona?"

"A message of sympathy, advising one of her favourite potions, which she also sent, and complaints that I am too fond of fish, which she abhors!"

"You will not take the potion?" Blanche asked in alarm, and Fiona laughed.

"Do you think me a simpleton? But Katriona would not attempt to poison me so directly, for she could not escape suspicion. Oh, I also had a letter from Uncle Bruce. He says, though I know not whether to believe him, that he intends to come and visit me, bringing Donald."

"You think he might really bring the boy?"

"If he is in one of his better periods, he might. I am told that his mother was only mad at certain times during the first few years, and it seems as though Donald is the same, though poor Uncle Bruce cannot admit it is the same malady, and deceives himself into thinking the attacks are caused by other things, fevers, and such."

"Does he hope to make your cousin declare himself in person?"

"No doubt. I was too clearly not ready to listen to his father's embassy on his behalf. I do hope that they do not stay long."

Blanche echoed that hope when she met the young man. He was tall, but held himself with a stoop, one shoulder lower than the other, and his hands hanging loosely almost to his knees. His stare was disconcerting, and he shuffled along with an uneven gait. The whole effect was horrifying, and despite herself Blanche could barely repress a shudder whenever they met.

Strangely, his talk was lucid, and he knew a great deal about animals and birds. Apparently he spent much time watching them, but Blanche noticed that the dogs who inhabited the castle hall, and fought over the scraps, would never take any of the offerings Donald held out to them, waiting out of reach until, growing impatient, he tossed the bones to them, when they would pounce and scuttle away with their prize as fast as they could.

Blanche did her utmost to avoid him, but found it difficult since Donald appeared to be fascinated by her luxuriantly curling dark hair. He had, on the first meeting, stretched out his hand as if to stroke it, being called sharply to order by his father. Blanche took great care never to be alone where he might find her, especially when he took to shambling along after her. Alexander commented sardonically on his devotion to Blanche, much to her annoyance.

"Uncle Bruce must be careful, or our friend will be laying his heart and inheritance at the wrong feet," he murmured to Blanche one evening as he danced with her.

She glanced up at him in annoyance. "And no doubt you think I would accept!" she retorted.

"He will inherit a sizeable property, and

if you could bear to put up with him for a few years until he is hopelessly insane, you would be in control. If you were clever you could have a son and rule for him."

"How horrible!" she exclaimed. "Another poor mad child!"

"Oh, I do not suggest that Donald should father it," he said, laughing at her. "You could easily avoid his attentions, and choose a mate more to your liking. There would be no lack of candidates for the honour!"

Furious, Blanche broke away from him and went to stand near one of the fires. He followed, and conversed blandly on innocuous topics to the group about the fire, while Blanche seethed inwardly, waiting only for a chance to escape to her room. After a time the opportunity came when Fiona indicated that she wished to retire, and Blanche left with her. Having helped Fiona into bed she went along the passage towards her own room. As she turned a corner she halted abruptly. A door in front of her was open and Donald's voice, rather whining and unmistakable, floated out to her.

"But I prefer the other one, Father."

Blanche hesitated, wondering whether he would see her if she passed the open door, and heard Bruce reply.

"You cannot have her, my son. But we will persuade your cousin to accept you. There are ways of compromising her so that she will have no alternative. Once she is committed you can have the other girl too, but first we must secure your cousin."

Blanche turned and ran, heedless of the noise she made, back along the way she had come. Outside Fiona's room, where a guard had been stationed as was customary, she found Alexander talking in low tones to the man.

"I must speak with you," she gasped, and he looked at her in surprise.

"Come," he said briefly, leading her into a nearby room. "Now, what ails you?" he demanded as he guided her to a stool.

Breathlessly she told him what she had heard. To her chagrin he burst out laughing.

"Do you not believe me?"

"It is too ridiculous! Oh, I believe you

heard this scheme being hatched, but they could never carry it out. My dear cousin is guarded night and day, and no-one can harm her."

"But you will take extra care, please?" Blanche pleaded.

"Against two crazy fools? I must think his father as deranged as Donald to think that such a plan might work." He laughed again, and Blanche, angry at the thought that she might have been too credulous, bade him a frosty farewell and turned to leave the room. She found him beside her, opening the door.

"I will escort you to your room," he said, and she bridled at the mockery in his voice.

"I need no escort of yours!"

"But I, in the absence of your brother, consider it part of my duty to safeguard the honour as well as the persons of all in my charge," he responded, laughter in his voice.

Blanche submitted in silence, and merely nodded her thanks when they reached her door. Alexander caught her hand and bowed low over it, kissing it for what Blanche, hot with embarrassment, thought an inordinate length of time.

"So young Donald has some taste," she heard Alexander say softly after he had released her hand and she was able to escape from him and close her door.

6

THE next few days passed with agonising slowness to Blanche. She watched and waited with apprehension for an attack on Fiona by Bruce and Donald, at the same time being careful to keep as much out of Donald's way as possible. Blanche knew from Fiona that her uncle had again been attempting to persuade her to marry her cousin, pointing out that she would be in danger until she did marry, but the cousin himself had not approached her on his own behalf.

"What danger does he mean? Have you told him about the poisoned sweetmeats?"

"No," Fiona shook her head. "When I asked what he referred to he mentioned only Patrick's death, suggesting that whoever killed him might turn to me next."

"That does not sound as though he had aught to do with Patrick's death," Blanche said musingly.

"Unless he is deliberately trying to put me off the scent! I truly know not

131

what to believe!"

Father and son, having received an un-compromising rejection of their proposals from Fiona, which her uncle at last recognized as final, departed. Freed from her self-imposed restrictions, Blanche sought the peace of the terrace, deserted on this early October day, when there was a keen wind sweeping down from the hills. She pulled her fur lined cloak closely about her, gazing across at the forests where already the trees were losing their golden and russet leaves. Her solitude was soon disturbed when Alexander appeared, and as before stood beside her leaning on the wall.

"Are you disappointed?" he queried lazily, and she shot him a glance of annoyance.

"I am relieved that they did not make any attempt against Fiona," she said stiffly. "That is natural and should be obvious to you!"

"But I always thought a woman did not care to be proved wrong?" he said teasingly.

"I was not!" she protested. "I did hear them planning it! Just because they did not for some reason succeed does not prove me wrong! The guard was too effective, mayhap!"

"Do you always have an answer?" was his only reply.

"Do you have to torment me?"

"Torment? I have been led to believe, by the ladies of my acquaintance, that the topic of conversation they most enjoyed was themselves. I but sought to entertain you pleasantly."

Blanche looked up into his smiling face, for the moment speechless. No doubt he has known many women, he is so handsome, she thought irrelevantly. Then the unwavering gaze with which he was regarding her caused her to blush. Slowly the colour suffused her cheeks and, mortified, she turned away.

"Not all of us think of ourselves to the exclusion of other matters," she said, flinging up her head defiantly. "Methinks you do not know us as well as you would pretend. I bid you good day!"

She walked quickly away, his low laugh following her, her thoughts whirling, as she devised, too late, answers other than those she had given to his taunts.

Blanche contrived to avoid Alexander as much as possible during the next few days, conscious that he made her feel uncomfortable, but she forgot this when John returned, weary but triumphant from his mission. This time there was no need for secrecy, and Fiona called Blanche and Alexander into her sitting room while John reported on his journey.

"Well?" Fiona demanded when they had gathered about the cheerfully roaring flames. She smiled warmly at John as he leant against a settle beside the fire, staring down at her.

"My lady, my news is not very terrible. I had to travel a great deal, but I think I gained information about the fighting men of the Campbell clan who would support Duncan. I would estimate he can call on about three hundred men in all."

"Over a hundred more than I have," Fiona said in concern.

"Agreed, but your men have fought with Montrose. They are more experienced, and having fought together they know their limitations and their strengths. Many of Duncan's men are forced into service and would have no stomach for such a venture, unlike your Macdonalds who would be protecting their chieftain. I would expect many of the Campbells to be resentful, preferring to be cultivating their lands. He would have great fear of deserters."

"You underestimate clan loyalty," Alexander remarked, but while John's lips tightened, Fiona ignored him.

"Then you do not think we face much danger from him?" she asked hopefully.

"I do not say that. He is a dangerous man. But I doubt that he can field a dangerous force against the Macdonalds. I will arrange at once to send men I can trust to watch the borders between your lands and his. If he moves against us we will have adequate warning."

"And we will be on our guard here for any moves within," Alexander added. "I will now hand back my duty as Fiona's protector, Sir John. Fiona, I have not mentioned it earlier, but now your gallant steward is returned I must visit my own home. There is much there that needs my attention. Have I your leave?"

"You scarce need to ask. Truly, Alex, I am most grateful to you for your aid. I have been selfish keeping you here, when your home must call. After your long years of fighting you must be anxious to go there."

He smiled at her, inclining his head in acknowledgment of her thanks.

"I would not leave you and all I hold dear were it not important, cousin. As it is, I do not intend to remain more than a short while, long enough to put in train certain changes I have in mind."

Blanche wondered abstractedly what changes these could be, then firmly told herself that they were no concern of hers, and listened to the questions the others were asking John. He had obtained a great deal of information and seemed not to have aroused any suspicions. They talked late that night, and on leaving Alexander bent low over Fiona's hand.

"I propose to depart early so I will bid you farewell now, cousin. I shall be gone before you rise. Be careful, do not exert yourself too greatly, for you are still not fully recovered from your illness."

"Farewell to you, Alex. I will be careful."

John had looked quickly from one to the other while this brief exchange took place, but he could not demand an explanation

136

then. He waited until Blanche left Fiona, and then accompanied her to her apartments.

"What illness is this?" he asked abruptly.

Blanche hesitated, wondering whether Fiona would prefer to tell John herself what had happened, and then, thinking that if he heard it directly from Fiona he might betray his feelings too clearly and embarrass them, she told him all she knew about the suspected poisoning attempt.

"Who else knows the truth?" he demanded brusquely.

"Janet and mother only. The physician may suspect, but we tried to throw the blame on fish we had eaten for supper. I pretended to be slightly indisposed too."

"What of Alexander? Does he know?"

"Fiona would not tell him. She felt that he might challenge Colin."

"Could she possibly suspect him?"

Blanche looked her astonishment. "He would not, surely? What could he gain? Colin and his four children stand between him and the chieftainship. He would do better to wed Fiona."

"Is not that what he intends? Though I cannot see that she favours him."

"I do not think she does," Blanche

agreed thoughtfully. "I have heard her say she would never marry him, and yet there are many pressures on her to marry. Alexander is a soldier and a strong man who would be able to protect her. There is much to be said for such a marriage," she concluded firmly, knowing that she was herself unconvinced.

John paced up and down restlessly, and Blanche eyed him with compassion. He could not show his love for Fiona, and must watch with complaisance her marriage with another man and, if she chose Alexander, to one he disliked. At last John turned to her.

"Watch over her for me when I cannot be there," he said simply, and Blanche went to hug him tightly.

"Of course, for I love her too."

John smiled a brief acknowledgment and then left her, but Blanche could not sleep for hours that night, wondering what the outcome for them all would be.

The next few days, with Alexander away, were oddly dull. Blanche admitted to herself that, angry as her occasional clashes with him had made her at the time, she missed the stimulation of his presence.

Fiona had now completely recovered from her illness, and was once more busy with the affairs of her inheritance. She frequently rode out, saying that she wanted to make the most of the autumn before winter closed its icy grip on the Highlands. One morning, when it promised to be a warm and sunny day, she called Blanche and said that she had a yearning to go hunting.

"I have arranged a small party, Blanche. Change into your habit, and we will have some fine sport."

"Is John coming?" Blanche asked, for he normally insisted on accompanying them when they rode out.

"No, he has gone to see about a fight there was last night amongst some of the clansmen, over disputed land, I think. There are several unclaimed farms, and whenever one person wishes to occupy some deserted farm, you can be sure at least two others will say that they have a prior claim, and it is the best of the land available."

"Alexander said to take care," Blanche reminded her.

"Oh, what of it? He has no right to

order me about, none whatsoever. Besides, I do not intend to go far, or away from my own lands. Shall we ride along the Bishop's valley?"

Blanche was tempted. She loved this particular valley, with its narrow entrance opening through a high gorge in the hills, once defended by the castle of a bishop. Inside the valley widened into a bowl shaped depression, not deep, but with no easy access apart from the gorge at one end and a narrow path beside a small but fast running river at the far end, through a further range of hills. In the floor of the valley the river wound peacefully through forest land and there was an abundance of deer.

"I think we ought to remain nearer home," she said doubtfully.

"It may be the last time we can reach it before the snow comes and cuts it off completely," Fiona said persuasively. "Do let us go today."

Blanche felt compelled to protest, but Fiona was determined, seeming especially to resent the advice that Alexander had proffered before his departure. Suppressing her worry that neither John nor Alexander

140

could accompany them, Blanche had to content herself with the sight of a dozen sturdy men, mostly nearby landowners, but with a couple of the richer townsmen too, that made up the party.

They rode off gaily, Fiona in the lead, and Blanche found herself riding beside one of the younger men that she had known for some time. He was gallantly attentive, and she could read the admiration in his eyes, but although she smiled at him she rather bleakly thought to herself that she did not feel any more warmly towards him than to anyone else. John had told her a few days earlier that Roger Grant, the man to whom he was hoping to marry her, had written that he would come to Scotland in the following spring, and he was sure that all could be arranged so that the wedding could take place within a short time. If all went as planned Blanche would be returning to England with him the following summer. This would be the last autumn she would have in Scotland.

Blanche wondered now, as she replied lightly to her companion's compliments, whether she would ever love a man. So far she had known nothing of that emotion, and although she knew that she would be expected to love this man who would become her husband, she could not help longing to experience something akin to the feelings she saw that John had for Fiona, hopeless though they seemed of fulfilment.

They rode for the valley, a few miles away from the castle, and Blanche shivered involuntarily as they passed in single file along the path through the gorge. On the one side was a steep drop to the silvery river, foaming as it rushed below along its narrow, rock-strewn bed: on the other a sheer rockface was surmounted by the ruined but still imposing castle of the long dead bishop. No attackers could have forced that entrance, for the defenders could have pushed them down into the deadly river with ease, simply by casting down rocks from above.

Once through the gorge, however, the river was gentle and inviting, with mossy banks bordering its still, deep, dark pools, and the bright shallows where the water sparkled and gurgled, wending its merry way. The trees were mixed firs and oaks, and there were many enchanting glades that Blanche wanted to stop and explore.

They hunted for a couple of hours with little success, and then halted in one of the glades beside the river to eat the food they had brought with them. It was warm for the time of year, here in the sheltered valley, and the beauty of the scene attracted them more than the chase for some time, so that they lingered beside the river. At length, with a regretful sigh, Fiona made a move to leave.

"We must return, I fear, for it grows dark early. We can make another cast as we go back down the valley, and mayhap 'twill be more successful than earlier."

They agreed, and the men began to saddle up the horses which had been tethered under the shade of the trees, when suddenly the sound of riders thrusting through the forest was heard. Before anyone could do more than utter a startled exclamation, they found themselves surrounded by at least twice as many horsemen, brandishing dirks and guns threateningly.

"Drop your guns and you will receive no hurt," Fiona's men were ordered brusquely by a man who rode slightly in front of the rest of the band.

There was no alternative, since they were covered with pistols and had been utterly unprepared. The leader of the band of men smiled grimly to see his orders obeyed, then leapt from his horse, throwing the reins to another man.

"My lady chieftain," he said, approaching Fiona. "I intend you no harm if you do not resist. I have orders to conduct you to my master who wishes to talk with you on a matter that closely concerns you both."

"And who might that be?" Fiona demanded angrily. "I have no wish to talk with one who conveys his requests in such an unmannerly way!"

The fellow shrugged, and eyed her insolently.

"You are in little case to refuse. As to his name, I am not at liberty to disclose that as yet. Let us not waste further time. We have far to go this day."

One of the men in Fiona's party stepped forward and began to protest, but he was immediately seized by two of the attackers and cord was tied about his arms.

"You can do nought," he was told as he was roughly pushed to one side. "We take the lady, and we will take your mounts. It should not be too long a walk home for you."

He grasped Fiona by the arm, but she angrily threw him off.

"Take your filthy hands off me, you scoundrel! For the moment you are successful and I must accompany you, but do not dare to touch me!"

"Which is your horse?" he asked, with a grin at her.

"The grey."

"Saddle it," the man ordered, and one of his men hastened to obey.

Blanche took a couple of steps forward and the leader turned towards her, waving her back. She ignored him and went closer, her head high, until she halted a mere pace away.

"The Lady Fiona has recently been ill and needs a woman to tend her, especially if you mean to ride far," she said calmly. "You must take me too."

"No, Blanche! You do not know what they will do!" Fiona cried out anxiously.

"They must take me," Blanche asserted. "I cannot leave you alone with them."

"Aye, let's take the wench," one of

the other men said, and a companion sniggered.

"Why not? Our master will have his sport with my lady, why not take the other for us, Rob?"

Blanche shivered, but did not allow her gaze to leave the leader's face. He stared back, and then nodded.

"Why not? Get her horse too then. And hasten."

Fiona still protested but Blanche ignored her pleas. They were flung up into the saddles and then, surrounded by their captors who also led the remaining horses belonging to Fiona's friends, were taken further up the valley.

After an hour's riding they came to the far end, where the river, very much smaller now, entered through a narrow gap in the hills. This was not a gorge as lower down the valley, but the path was as narrow. It climbed steeply beside the river which flowed rapidly down its course, tumbling over the rocks and waterfalls in its way. Several times they had to dismount and pull the horses along the steeper parts, and it was almost dusk when they came out onto the higher but flatter land above.

Now they made much better speed, riding with the sun behind them, sinking fast behind the ranges of hills further away towards the sea. After half an hour they began descending another valley, and here it was dark amongst the trees. Blanche shivered apprehensively. She had rarely been out in the forests in darkness, and as the trees loomed above her, silent and menacing, she thought fearfully of the many tales she had heard of witches and demons, giants and wolves that inhabited these forests. Angrily she told herself that the tales were fantasies, made to frighten children, and the peril they were in from their captors was far greater than any other, but this provided scant comfort.

Since they had been captured the girls had been kept apart so that they could not talk, either to speculate on what lay before them, or keep high one another's spirits. Fiona was in front, and occasionally her shadow was recognizable as the lantern the leader now carried to guide them swung about.

For some time they had been descending, but now the ground seemed to be sloping upwards again. Then Blanche realised that the stars were visible, and they had emerged from the shelter of the trees. A vast shape, a tall square tower, loomed up before them, a more solid shadow in the almost total darkness of their surroundings, and they were led towards it. A narrow gateway was revealed, and before it the men dismounted. In the light of the single lantern Blanche could now see that there was but a single plank spanning a ditch which had once been a moat, but which, for lack of maintenance, was now dry.

Stiff with the long ride, the girls were helped to dismount, and their horses led away. They were guided across the plank into the small courtyard before the tower. By now a faint moon had arisen and the walls were discernible in its light, though little else could be distinguished. The men seemed to know their way about, however, and those who had not disappeared with the horses rapidly built a fire and prepared a rough camp.

As they did not seem unduly concerned with the girls, Blanche moved across to where Fiona had seated herself on a fallen stone, part of the inner wall of the tower, and sat beside her.

"I am grateful, but could wish that you had not put yourself into this danger," Fiona whispered to her, reaching for her hand and holding it tightly.

"I could not leave you. Besides, we might find some way of escape," Blanche said, more in an attempt to comfort her than from any real hope of this. "Do you know where we are?"

"Yes. We are near the river that separates Macdonald and Campbell lands. Duncan's lands are on the far side. The valley we followed has a small river that joins the main one."

"Then Duncan is responsible for this outrage."

Fiona was silent.

"Who else could it be?" Blanche asked in some surprise, realizing that Fiona did not seem certain.

"I cannot be certain. Several of the men are wearing Campbell tartans, but that proves little. You see, I recognized one of the men. He is Alex's servant."

"What? Can you think him responsible?" Blanche asked incredulously.

"I do not know. It seemed suspicious that he was away from me just now, and his home lies on this river, further towards the sea. We might be heading there instead of to Duncan."

"So that he can force you to marry him?"

"I never will!" Fiona declared vehemently. "Especially not if he is responsible for this!"

Their talk was interrupted as the leader of the men came across to them. He carried a lantern and a roll of bedding.

"Follow me," he ordered curtly and they rose to do so.

Leading the way towards the tower wall he guided them through a narrow door and down some rough steps into a small room below the ground.

"You will sleep in here. We will be above, so do not think to escape. Food will be brought."

To their relief he left the lantern, and they set about making a bed out of the blankets he had dropped beside them and their own cloaks. It was now very cold, and they were glad to huddle together under the makeshift covers while they waited for the food. When it came it was warm and appetising, and they ate it hungrily, and drank the wine from the bottle left with them. Then, their plates having been removed, and the door barred, they were left in peace.

Outside the men were gathered round the fire, singing lustily, obviously having plenty to drink.

"The door is not very strong. Can we force it open after they sleep?" Fiona whispered.

"They will be immediately above, and even if they do not leave a guard we could not creep past them."

"They might all be asleep after they have finished carousing," Fiona said hopefully, but Blanche shook her head.

"I wonder if there is any other way out of here?" she said, and picking up the lantern began to prowl round the small room with it.

The door was barred on the far side, and the only other opening was a slit of a window high in the thick stone wall, and far too narrow for them to squeeze through. Despondently Blanche set down the lantern and threw herself onto the bedding.

"We might escape them tomorrow," she

151

said, though with little conviction.

"When we know where they take us I will be in a position to bargain, with either Duncan or Alex. There is a possibility that they would believe that a forced marriage would not be accepted by the rest of my family. At least I can thank their greed for that! Uncle Colin would not permit his hopes to be dashed in such a manner. I might bargain with him, whoever it is, and be allowed to go free so that a marriage would appear to be made of my own free will. And when I am free John will protect me!" she finished fiercely.

"It could work," Blanche agreed.

"If I begin to make unlikely promises, do not be afraid. I do not mean to abide by them when they are forced from me in this manner!"

They lay silently, watching the shadows cast by the lantern, and listening to the singing men outside.

"This floor is hard," Blanche complained after a while, and rose to try and rearrange the blankets more comfortably. As she shook them she paused, then bent to look more closely at the earth floor on which they lay.

"What is it?" Fiona asked.

"Hush! What I was lying on, and what was hard, is a metal ring, almost covered with earth. And look here, it lifts a trapdoor! Can you see where I have scraped away the earth, there is a gap between the door and the frame that holds it?"

The girls looked at one another with rising hope. This might be a way out of their prison. They scraped away to reveal the whole of the trapdoor, and Blanche tentatively pulled at the ring. It gave after a few tugs, and the door began to lift.

"We must wait," Fiona warned. "Let us cover the lantern so that if they look in on us they will think we have put it out and are asleep. When they are abed we will explore."

It seemed hours to the anxious girls before the revellers outside were silent. Then, fear mingled with hope, they lifted the trapdoor fully to reveal a steep, uneven flight of steps twisting away into the depths.

7

BLANCHE seized the lantern and stepped towards the hole. She peered down it, Fiona close beside her.

"We must try," Fiona said, and Blanche nodded, turned to pick up her cloak, and then began the descent.

The stairs twisted away, and the many cobwebs witnessed to the disused state of them. Though uneven the stairs were firm, and the girls counted fourteen steps before reaching a short passageway that ended in a small, stout wooden door only a few feet away.

"It opens away from the courtyard, I am sure!" Blanche exclaimed excitedly, and they looked at one another with rising hope.

Fiona stepped forward and lifted the latch. She pulled, and with a protesting creak the door swung open. Blanche let out a sigh, and they both peered eagerly through the opening. Here the lantern gave them small illumination, but the moon enabled them to see that they had opened a small postern door in the outer wall of the tower, and only a few feet below them was a dry ditch that had once been the moat.

"We had best leave the lantern, for it could betray us," Fiona said, and she blew out the light. Then, making as little noise as they could, they slid down the steep side to the bottom of the ditch, and scrambled with some difficulty up the much higher outer side. Blanche noticed with relief that the plank bridge they had crossed earlier was not on this side of the castle, but there might still be guards posted.

"Into the trees while we decide what to do," she whispered, and they ran for the shelter of a grove of trees nearby.

Pausing, they listened anxiously for signs of alarm or pursuit, but all was silent. Recalling her terror of the forest they had passed through earlier that night, Blanche almost laughed to think that now she was welcoming the protection of the dark concealing trees.

"Can we get the horses, do you think?" she asked.

"We will try. They were led away

somewhere outside the tower. If not, we must walk."

"But you are unfit to walk far so soon after your illness," Blanche protested worriedly. "We might soon be able to obtain horses from a farmer."

Fiona remained silent, knowing how very unlikely this was in the wild country where they found themselves, but unwilling to discourage Blanche at the outset.

"We are almost on the river that borders Campbell land," she began explaining. "We followed another, smaller river valley that joins it. This area is full of such valleys. I suggest that instead of retracing our steps up the same valley, which is the first way the men will look for us, and which leads us across the hills into the Bishop's valley where no-one lives, we go further up the main river and follow another side valley that I know. Once over the hills we ought soon to come to farms."

"They might search there too," Blanche commented. "Is there anywhere we could hide when day comes?"

"Yes, there are many caves in the sides of the hills. They could not possibly search all of them."

"Then let us go."

Carefully they crept through the trees towards the place where the horses had been tethered for the night. The occasional jingle of a bit or snort of a restless horse guided them, but their disappointment was great when they saw that the horses had been placed within the walls of what had once been a chapel, but which had lost its roof long ago. At the only doorway they could see two guards and hear their quiet talk. There was no hope of getting mounts for the long and difficult journey that lay ahead of them.

Stealing softly back the way they had come, they suppressed their dismay. Fiona, who knew the lie of the land, led the way in a circuitous route around the tower and down towards the rough track that wound beside the turbulent river. Keeping in the shelter of the trees as much as possible they began to walk steadily southwards, alert for any sounds that would indicate other travellers, their captors or anyone else, and prepared to run for the nearest cover if necessary.

The night was cold, and they pulled their cloaks tightly about them, trying to keep out the chill breezes that blew from the water. Blanche watched Fiona closely for signs of fatigue, but she seemed unaffected by her adventures and the lack of sleep. Her step was sprightly, and she commented frequently upon the beauty of the night, and the occasional movements of birds or night animals that they heard. It could have seemed that she had deliberately chosen to explore part of her domain by night with but another girl as sole companion and protector.

After walking for an hour or so they came to the valley Fiona had decided to follow.

"The main path is on the far side of this little river," she said, pointing across. "Normally we could ford the river and ride up that side, but there is another, smaller path on this side, and we had best follow that. The men are more likely to search the far side."

"But they will know we did not cross," Blanche objected. "The water is too deep and cold without horses."

"Then they may think we did not come this way at all, except that there is a small village here, and several small boats moored on this side of the river. It would not have been too difficult for us to have crossed unseen."

"Should we not try to obtain help, or at least shelter, at one of the cottages? They are Macdonald clansmen, are they not?"

Fiona shook her head decidedly. "We cannot seek their aid. They would have no reason to believe me, and I doubt if any of them have ever seen me, for they live a solitary life here. Besides, if Alex was responsible for capturing us, these people would obey him, since his own home is not far away, and he is their overlord. And if Duncan is responsible, they know that he would take swift revenge on any that thwarted him, and his lands are just across the main river. They have suffered from him in the past and would not help us if they knew he might be involved."

By now the moon was setting and it was more difficult for them to find their way, but they skirted the cottages, with only a single bark from a dog in an outhouse to indicate that they were perceived. The track beside the river was narrow, but smooth and well worn for some way out of the village, passing several tiny walled fields where cattle were penned, then giving way to uncultivated hillside covered with heather and bracken.

After a while the going became much rougher, and they had to walk more slowly to avoid the holes in the path. They were guided mainly by the faint gleams on the river and its gurgling as it ran over the rocky bed. For an hour they stumbled cautiously on, and at last greeted with relief the first threads of light that heralded the dawn.

Now they were able to move faster, and they hurried, knowing that the further they could get before they needed to rest and hide during the day, the safer they would be from their attackers. Looking back along the valley, Blanche gasped at the sight before her. She was looking directly into the sunrise, and its orange glow illuminated the silver river with flames flickering over the surface. The valley was bathed in a soft light and a thin mist veiled the hills to either side. No humans were in sight, but a few sheep roamed the hillside.

"How lovely it is," she breathed softly.

"Apart from some of its inhabitants,"

Fiona said with a wry laugh.

"Will they be following us yet, I wonder?"

"They will discover our escape at daylight. About now, let us suppose. Even if they come this way at once it would take them an hour or more to catch up with us. We can go on for that long at least. And further up the valley the going is much more difficult for horsemen. If we can reach the higher parts we can see anyone following. In perhaps two hours we ought to stop. We shall then be near a number of caves and we can hide in one of them. We must find one that will give us a view of the valley."

They went on, more slowly now as the way grew steeper, and Blanche was concerned to see that Fiona's steps were flagging. She walked slowly, with a dragging step, and halted frequently to breathe deeply. At last they came to a wilder place still, where the slopes of the valley were steep, scattered with rocks, and pitted with hollow depressions and deeper caves. Here they must remain, to rest and for fear of pursuit.

They drank their fill of the icy cold water, although the river was little more than a trickle this far up the valley. Hungry after their exertions, they wished that they had food, but there was none to be had, and they retreated to a cave high up from the river, its entrance partly hidden from the path below by thorn bushes, but with a good view down the valley.

"You must sleep if you can," Blanche said firmly. "I will watch and wake you if there is any movement."

"You need sleep also," Fiona protested. "Wake me after two hours and I will take my turn at watching."

Blanche nodded, resolving not to obey, for she was deeply concerned at the dark circles round Fiona's eyes and her pallor. Deciding that it was better not to argue, she set about collecting as much heather as she could find nearby, and contriving a bed with it. Fiona subsided onto it with a deep sigh, and despite the discomfort was soon fast asleep. Blanche sat with her back against a boulder, huddled into her cloak, where she could watch the valley but be unseen herself, and began to consider who could have been responsible for their abduction.

How had anyone known where they

would be found that day, she wondered. It had been a sudden decision on Fiona's part to hunt in the Bishop's valley. How could Duncan have known of that and prepared an attack? It was always possible that one of Fiona's servants had betrayed her, but would Duncan have taken the risk of starting a conflict between his clan and hers, when she had sent back an answer that could have given him hope that in the end she would accept his suit? Blanche thought it unlikely. The presence of the man Fiona had recognised as Alexander's servant seemed to point to him as the perpetrator of the deed. His departure from the castle could be explained by his need to organise such a plot, and he would not have shown himself amongst the attackers to prevent news of his involvement being taken back to Fiona's people. The more Blanche considered it, the more she became convinced that Alexander was responsible, and she fumed helplessly. He had always been determined to marry Fiona, she thought, recalling the many times he had referred to it, despite Fiona's uncompromising rejection of the idea.

Gloomily Blanche watched the valley, but

all remained peaceful. She was exhausted by the riding of the previous day, followed by the long walk and the sleepless night, and had great difficulty in keeping awake, but with occasional walks about the cave, taking care to keep out of sight of anyone in the valley, she contrived to stay awake until the sun was high in the sky, and the mouth of the cave, facing eastwards, had just slipped into shadow.

Soon afterwards Fiona stirred, and stretched herself stiffly. She groaned as she sat up, but Blanche thankfully noticed that there was more colour in her cheeks.

"You have let me sleep too long!" she exclaimed, noticing the position of the sun as she came to the cave entrance.

"You are still unwell, and need rest," Blanche replied.

"I have had it, and I am now so stiff I never wish to lie on that bed again! It is your turn, Blanche, for you must be weary!"

"Indeed I am," Blanche confessed, and after reporting that she had seen nothing throughout the morning, she stretched thankfully on the makeshift bed and immediately fell asleep.

It was dusk when Fiona gently shook her awake.

"They will not venture so far up the valley so late in the day," she explained. "We can risk moving now, and as we are so near the head of the valley we might be able to reach the one on the far side of the hills before it is too dark to see our way. In a few hours we can go on by moonlight and before tomorrow morning we ought to find a safe house where we can ask for help. It will be welcome, for I am ravenous!" she concluded, and Blanche, her own hunger intense after a foodless day, agreed that they ought to set off without delay.

Now the way was much steeper, and the river disappeared entirely. They were climbing towards a shoulder of bare land stretching between two afforested hilltops, and there was only the faintest of tracks to guide them. Deer grazing on the open turf raised their heads in alarm at this unusual invasion, and swiftly bounded back into the sheltering woods. Rabbits, less timid, merely skittered further away and returned to their feeding.

"I wish I could eat grass," Fiona commented with a faint laugh.

Blanche nodded, and suggested that they would soon find help in the valley beyond the shoulder, though thinking dismally that it seemed as far away as it had half an hour before, when they had set out.

Eventually they reached the summit, to see stretching away yet another slope similar to the one they had just crossed. But this time it was downwards, and with rather more buoyancy in their steps they began the descent. Soon it was too dark to go on safely, for there were many rocks covering the hillside. They found shelter amongst a clump of trees and crouched down close together, shivering from the bitter cold while they waited for the moon to rise.

Fiona had dozed, and slumped against Blanche who sat with her arms cradled about her friend. She wondered whether they would be able to go on, but knew that they would not survive a night spent motionless in the open, in such cold, and in their weakened, hungry state. Regretfully she wakened Fiona, who struggled up and smiled courageously.

"Not much longer before we reach help," she said, attempting a gay tone.

They walked for what seemed hours, gradually slowing their pace, then forced to take frequent rests. After a time they came to the stream that flowed through this valley, and they followed it, noticing how swiftly it grew wider and deeper. But long before the moon set they had to admit that they could walk no further until they had slept again. Fortunately there were more caves here, and they stumbled into one, too tired to collect heather for a bed, and lay utterly exhausted, sleeping until dawn.

"We cannot afford to wait here all day," Blanche declared, seriously concerned at Fiona's haggard looks. "If those men were going to search these valleys they would have done so yesterday. We must go on and find food and help as soon as possible."

Fiona nodded, and wearily they set off again. Soon, to Blanche's joy, they saw a hut in the distance. Their steps quickening, they went towards it, but realised as they came nearer that it had long been deserted.

"It is often the case with these hill farms," Fiona explained, fighting to keep back her tears of weakness and disappointment. "So much of the land has been devastated in past years by raids from other clans that the farmers have moved nearer to the villages for greater protection."

"Let us hope that not all the farmers have gone," Blanche commented grimly. "Rest here, and I will at least look to see if there is anything we can eat."

She went on what she feared would be a hopeless mission, for the hut had a long-neglected air about it, but in the kitchen she came across a skin bottle, and it was full of rough but palatable whisky. That would give them some strength, at least, she thought, and ran back to Fiona with her find. They drank the fiery spirit, and feeling warmer and much more hopeful went on their way. The valley was much narrower here and often the river ran through steep gorges. Usually they were able to find a way round on the higher ground above, but on more than one occasion they had to wade through the water, which was icy cold but fortunately not deep.

They were in one of these places, wading through with their skirts held high, and their shoes slung round their necks, when Fiona slipped on a sharp stone and fell, gasping as she stretched full length in the icy water. She scrambled up quickly, and Blanche helped her to wade through the stream until they could climb out onto the bank. Fiona was shivering violently, and without ceremony Blanche began stripping off the wet clothes. Then she used her own cloak to rub Fiona briskly until she was dry, and made her sit with her arms round her knees while she spread the cloak over her.

"Oh, I am a fool!" Fiona exclaimed, still shivering.

"Not in the least. You are lightheaded with lack of food, and the whisky did not help that! The sun is warm, thank heavens, and will soon dry your gown, and then we can go on."

They rested for an hour, and then, despite Fiona's protests Blanche forced her to put on her own dry gown while she donned the still damp one Fiona had been wearing.

"I shall take no harm, but you have been ill. Wear my cloak too, and I will carry yours so that as we walk the sun will dry the gown still more."

They passed three more farmhouses, all

deserted, and none of them yielded up any food or drink, so that all they had was water from the river. At last, outside the third house, Fiona sat down on the grass and put her head in her hands and wept.

"I cannot go on! I must sleep first! Let us stay here until morning."

Blanche glanced anxiously at the sun. It was high in the sky and only midday.

"Do you think we are within reach of any habitation where there are people?" she asked.

"There is a small village, but it is an hour's walk or more. I cannot make any further effort. Mayhap after a sleep I can try. There should be someone there."

"Then I will go and fetch help. You can rest here."

Weakly Fiona agreed. "Follow the river," she said, and made no protest when Blanche led her into the farmhouse and made a couch for her to lie on from some straw she found.

Desperately anxious by now Blanche went on alone. She knew that if she did not find help soon Fiona would be likely to die of exposure. She prayed feverishly as she struggled along, her own steps faltering in her weakness, and only kept going by her fierce determination not to be beaten by their enemies.

So dazed and weary was she that she did not see the rider approaching, and did not hear as he exclaimed in amazement and leapt from his saddle. The first she knew was when an arm was slipped round her to support her and, vaguely aware that this was unexpected, she halted.

"My God! You are soaking wet! Where is your cloak?"

She lifted her head, painfully, and perceived Alexander gazing down into her eyes. A nameless fear possessed her, and she began to struggle.

"No, you must not! Go away! I will not tell you where she is!"

Grimly he swung her up onto his horse, and mounted behind her. Her struggles were feeble and he held her with ease, unwinding his plaid so that he could wrap the end round her as well. Then he turned his horse and cantered back down the valley. Blanche dimly realised which direction they were going in and cried out in alarm.

"Fiona! Let me! I must get back to her!"

"When you are safe," he replied soothingly, and soon halted and dismounted before a small cottage which stood with an open, welcoming door, and a glowing fire within.

Carrying Blanche inside he set her down unceremoniously before the fire, and as ruthlessly as she had previously stripped this same gown from Fiona, he stripped it from her. She was too weak to protest, and thankfully felt the warmth of a sheepskin rug on her skin as he wrapped it round her. Then he led her to a bed set in an alcove and forced her to lie on it. Blanche was just conscious enough to be aware of a woman hovering in the background and of Alexander turning to receive a tankard of warm broth from her. Slipping his arm beneath Blanche's shoulders, he raised her slightly and helped her to sip the broth. She felt its warmth course through her, and her consciousness returned. All her instinctive suspicions of him had disappeared, and her only thoughts were of rescuing Fiona.

"She is in a farmhouse, you must hurry!" she gasped, catching at the hand that held the broth, and almost causing him to spill it.

"You may have had sufficient, but that is no cause for wasting it!" he murmured in mocking reproof.

"Fiona!" she exclaimed.

"Hush, I will go for her now. You are in safe hands and will be looked after. Where is she?"

Blanche explained as well as she could, and he nodded and left. The woman, whose cottage it was, persuaded Blanche to have more broth, and then she fell fast asleep. It was dark when she awoke, and the cottage was illuminated by a single candle. The woman and her husband sat either side of the fire, she spinning and he carving a spoon from a piece of wood. Seeing Blanche stir, the woman laid aside the spindle and came across to the bed.

"How do you feel now?" she asked.

"Oh, much better, I thank you, but where is he?"

"Lord Alexander? He went to fetch his cousin and rode straight back to the castle with her, saying she needed the physician's attentions at once."

"Is she very ill?" Blanche asked worriedly.

"No. He said particularly that you were not to be concerned, and that he would be back for you as soon as possible. I would think he should arrive within the hour."

She prepared more broth for Blanche, who was exceedingly hungry, and ate heartily of cold beef and oatcakes. She was worried, her former suspicions of Alexander returning in full force, and fretted in case she had merely delivered Fiona back into the hands of her abductor. There was no more that she could do, however, except wait. In the morning, with the help of these people, who seemed loyal to Fiona, she could raise the alarm if it proved to be necessary.

"I have dried your gown, would you like to put it on before he returns?" the woman asked, and Blanche, suddenly recollecting that he had stripped it from her, blushed furiously and hastened to comply.

She had barely fastened the last lace when a knock came on the door and Alexander entered.

"Where is Fiona?" Blanche demanded without greeting him.

"Where do you expect?" he replied coolly. "At home, in Janet's care. Are you recovered sufficiently for the journey?"

"Yes, I thank you," she answered, subdued.

"Good, then we will ride. Here is another cloak. You appear to have lost yours."

"It was wet," Blanche replied absently, trying vainly to recall when she had last seen the cloak.

Alexander came across to her and placed the cloak about her shoulders, fastening it securely.

"You will ride pillion behind me," he said after she had thanked the cottagers who had cared for her, and was walking to the door.

"Alone?" she asked, startled, and halted in the doorway.

He laughed. "No. Your suspicious brother sent a couple of men to chaperone us!"

Blanche ignored his mocking tone. "Then John is back? What has been happening?"

He told her as they rode along that the remnants of the hunting party had struggled back to the castle as dusk was falling. A party of men had set off immediately to search the Bishop's valley, but had had no success in the darkness. On the following day a larger company had ridden through to the other valley, and had found traces of the occupation of the ruined tower, but no clues as to where the men had gone. If any of the local farmers had seen them, they were not prepared to talk.

"Your brother arrived in the middle of the day and immediately sent all the available men off in detachments to search. I heard of it late last night and rode straight for the castle to discover the truth of it. No trace of you had been found, so I have been searching the valleys leading towards the river, hoping your abductors would be hiding there, or that you had contrived to escape them, and were making for home. What did happen?"

Blanche described their ordeal, and he made few comments, except to say that had he been there he would not have allowed Fiona to have been so foolhardy as to hunt with such a small party, so close to the Campbell lands.

"You have no authority," Blanche snapped. "Besides, it is not proved that Duncan was responsible."

"Really?" he drawled. "Who else do you think would be so impetuous? Or desperate!"

Blanche refused to reply, and he laughed softly.

"Oho! You suspect me, no doubt?"

"Since one of your men was amongst them, it is a reasonable suspicion!" she retorted recklessly.

"What do you think I had in mind? Murder or marriage?"

Regretting her previous outburst, Blanche firmly closed her lips. He chuckled.

"I have another plan, but as yet I do not intend to reveal what it is," he said calmly, and then relapsed into silence for the remainder of the journey.

The reactions to the outrage on Fiona were varied. The people were furious that their beloved chieftain had been so badly treated, and in danger, and vowed vengeance on her attackers. She had recovered speedily from the ordeal, but had to face those of a different nature when her uncles arrived, both scolding her for her lack of care and telling everyone who would listen that they had repeatedly warned her of the dangers. She bore their strictures in silence, but refused to discuss with them her suspicions about who was responsible. Relenting towards Colin when he remarked that her god-daughter, his youngest child Maria, was almost four years old and had not seen Fiona since her babyhood, she promised to pay him a visit two weeks later, and he departed content. Bruce, when he heard of the plan, demanded that Fiona also pay him a visit, and she wearily agreed, arranging to go on to him after her visit to Colin. When Alexander discovered these plans he rated Fiona for a simpleton.

"I will do precisely as I choose!" she flared at him. "Mayhap my uncles are more to be trusted than I have previously thought!"

Aggravatingly, he merely laughed, but she forgot her annoyance when entirely without warning the Black Duncan arrived at the castle.

He was displaying a great deal of injured innocence, complaining at the injustice of the rumours that pinned the abduction on him.

"How could I hope to win you by those means?" he asked. "You returned so favourable an answer to my embassy that I await your decision with quiet confidence. I came to press my suit less formally, to assure you that in your situation normal considerations need not apply. Your loss, when your betrothed was so unfortunate in suffering that accident, was not the same as the loss of your father. I would advise, for your safety as well as because it is my desire, that you marry with as much speed as possible."

"Patrick's death, whether it was an accident or no, greatly disturbed me," Fiona prevaricated.

"Oh, yes, you have heard rumours to the effect that I was responsible for that too, I see. Utterly ridiculous, of course, though my love for you, my dear, is far greater than is usual in a marriage of convenience, and could well drive me to do unwise deeds. I verily believe I would marry you were you a penniless waif! That being so, I would be very jealous of anyone else who pretended to your hand."

Fiona shivered, for the menace in those last words were very clear. They were sitting in the great hall, watching some tumblers, and she and Duncan sat slightly apart. She glanced round uneasily and Alexander, interpreting her glance, strolled elegantly across to engage Duncan in conversation so that Fiona could escape.

8

JOHN'S suspicions of Alexander were increasing, and he confided them to Blanche.

"He has had the opportunity for all the attacks, and no proof has been found against him or anyone else. Of them all he is the only one Fiona would ever consider marrying, so he has most to gain by ridding himself of Patrick."

"But he would not therefore poison her," Blanche objected.

"I cannot tell!" John paced worriedly up and down. "Anyone could have slipped a poisoned sweetmeat into that box, not only Colin. Mayhap it was not meant to kill, just to frighten, so that Fiona would be more willing to be persuaded by him. Or, if what I think is true, he might have been ruthless enough to contemplate killing Colin and all his children too!"

"John, that would be too much!" Blanche protested "No-one would believe them all to be accidents!"

"It has been done. The Highlands are wild, Blanche. But if only Colin were dead, he might claim the chieftainship by saying that his sons were not old enough to rule. There are so many possibilities!"

"You also suspect he abducted her?"

"How else explain that his man was in the party? He has refused to give any other reason for that, though I know Fiona has asked him. He must be growing impatient."

Blanche wondered how much of his suspicion was the result of jealousy, as he thought of a possible marriage between his adored Fiona and the hated Alexander, but she had to confess that she was herself uncertain of his innocence. Soon, however, they were all concerned with the promised visit to Colin. John begged Fiona to cancel the visit; Alexander ordered her not to go; and Janet declared that no-one should separate her from her duty and she would accompany her mistress if she had to crawl all her way on hands and knees.

"Beset by them all, I wish that I could abandon the whole idea!" Fiona confided in Blanche, half laughing, half angry.

"Why do you not? John is right in saying that your journey would be another opportunity for an attack or abduction. And Janet fears another poison attempt."

"If Colin or Katriona were responsible for the first one, they would never dare try again while I was with them," Fiona declared, but Blanche was unconvinced, and argued until Fiona laughingly promised that she would not eat or drink anything but what her aunt and uncle also tasted.

"Or what Janet prepares, for you will take her with you, will you not?" Blanche added, and Fiona nodded.

"We shall have so many guardians that Colin's house will be overflowing. He will not again press me to visit them so urgently!"

That night at supper, John, who was still unreconciled to the visit, again expressed his disquiet. Patiently Fiona repeated that the little Margaret had a right to know the cousin who was her chieftain as well as her god-mother.

"Then send for the child and have her here," Alexander said curtly. "You must not go."

"Must? You order me?" Fiona said

dangerously quietly, but her eyes glittering in anger.

"I say what everyone else thinks."

"But they advise, not order!"

"Your gallant steward agrees with me," Alexander pointed out.

"I but offer an opinion," John said stiffly, and Alexander laughed.

"And is it not a personal wish, as mine is?"

"My personal wishes are irrelevant," John said angrily, and Alexander gazed mockingly across the table at him.

Fiona intervened. "I appreciate that you both have my best interests in view," she said calmly, having mastered her anger. "I shall take several of my most trusted manservants with me, under you, John. Will you arrange to leave twenty or so to guard the castle? Does that content you both? Alex, I would ask you to remain in charge at the castle here. Now let there be no further argument, for my mind is quite made up."

When she spoke with such finality both men recognised the indomitable spirit of her father and capitulated. John nodded, but Alexander could not forbear to warn that she would regret it.

"Is that a threat?" she demanded, her anger rising to the surface again. As she grew angry, he grew correspondingly calm, and laughed mockingly.

"My dear cousin, I am well aware that your faithful steward here harbours the utmost suspicions of me, but I did not know that he had been so successful in poisoning your mind against me."

John, furiously angry, sprang to his feet, but a sharp word from Fiona made him bite back the words he had been about to fling at his tormentor. Fiona turned to Lady Emrey and made some remark to do with the welfare of one of the servants, and John sat back slowly, Alexander regarding him with some amusement from under discreetly lowered eyelids. The meal was completed in a strained atmosphere, and immediately afterwards John excused himself on the pretence of having preparations to make for the visit.

The next few days passed with the two young men in a state of almost open hostility, avoiding all but the most essential contacts, and Fiona confessed that she would be, thankful to get away from the castle so that they would be separated.

"When does your cousin return to his own home?" Blanche asked. "It is odd that he remains here."

Fiona shrugged. "I do not know what his plans are. He always spent a great deal of time here as a boy, for his mother died when he was born, and he had no brothers or sisters. Then he was not quite ten when his father was killed. He has always looked upon it as his home and has made no mention of what he plans to do now that the wars are over and he cannot go off soldiering. He has the most lovely castle, set high on a hillside and commanding two valleys. I hope that he means to settle down soon and live there."

They made their preparations and then, the day before they were due to start, Lady Emrey fell down some stairs and hurt her leg. Unable to walk, she needed company and attention, and Blanche insisted on staying behind with her, despite her mother's protests that there was no need. She waved goodbye to the cavalcade in the courtyard, then ran to the topmost battlements of the highest tower to watch the procession wind its way down the hill and through the town, where the townsfolk stood to wave to their chieftain, and then across the flat land beside the loch. It was a brave sight, with Fiona riding ahead of almost fifty of her clansmen, and the numerous baggage ponies bringing up the rear. The scarlet and green plaids of the men cut a swathe across the ground, where a light fall of snow had covered the grass and the heather. Shining in the weak winter sunlight, the swords of the men gleamed brightly, edging the mass of colour with glistening wetness, causing Blanche to think suddenly of blood. She shivered, and a deep chuckle came from behind her. Swinging round she saw Alexander leaning against the door that led to the stairs.

He unfastened his sheepskin jacket and strolled across to her, dropping it about her shoulders.

"You seem to make it a habit, going without cloaks," he said with a laugh, and Blanche grew confused as she recalled that time, when he had held her so closely to him on his horse.

She pulled the heavy jacket close about

her, grateful for the warmth, but spoke hurriedly.

"I had not really noticed the cold," she said in surprise. "I shivered because suddenly they looked like a gigantic wound, oozing blood."

"You are fanciful. But what did happen to your cloak that day?"

"I cannot remember. It was wet, and at first I carried it, but I was so tired I cannot remember half of what happened. I must have dropped it."

They continued to talk of trivial matters, and Blanche studied Alexander unobtrusively. He could be a most entertaining companion, she conceded, when he made the effort. Was he really the villain she half suspected?

The next week passed peacefully. Spending most of her time with her mother and taking her meals in her mother's apartments, Blanche saw very little of Alexander, but he seemed to appear whenever she walked on the terrace or climbed up to the tower, and she grew to look forward to these meetings, for by mutual unspoken consent they avoided all contentious topics and spent much time comparing life in England and Scotland. Alexander was steeped in the history of the Highlands and gave Blanche an enthusiasm for it that she had never before felt. She realised how enormously proud of his ancestors he was, and how passionately he felt about the continued independence of the clan. The only flaw in her enjoyment of these meetings was the thought that his friendliness might be assumed in order to disarm her.

One morning Blanche had been walking for almost half an hour on the terrace and Alexander had not joined her, which was odd, for however she varied the time of these airings and wherever she went he always seemed to know and come to her. She felt an unreasonable sense of disappointment, mingled with chagrin, and chided herself for being taken in by pleasant manners and a handsome face. But the feeling persisted, and she determined to climb the tower. She told herself sternly that she was not looking for him, but the view from the terraces was limited, whereas from the tower one could see in all directions.

What she did see when she emerged onto

the battlements was totally unexpected. Normally one of the men patrolled the tower as a look-out, but today there were four up there, each one facing in a different direction.

"What is it?" she exclaimed, and the one nearest turned to her with a grim smile of greeting.

"Look down there, beyond the walls," he said, nodding towards the landward side of the castle.

Blanche approached the parapet and looked over. Circling the town, encamped a few hundred yards outside the walls, were dozens and dozens of men. Pack ponies were being led towards them in long lines, roped together, and when their cargoes were unloaded the men set to erecting rough shelters, hides stretched over sticks thrust into the ground. A couple of small cannon were being pulled into positions where they were pointing directly at the main gateway of the town, and already men were busy digging trenches leading towards the walls.

The town walls were black with citizens watching these ominous preparations, and at intervals Blanche could see the gleam of a sword, but these were pitiably few and she realised that there were only twenty of Fiona's men left in the castle to defend it and the town.

"Where is Al — Lord Alexander?" she asked, having absorbed all the horror of the scene before her.

"In the town, recruiting men to help with the defences," the man beside her said. "We have ample provisions and all the spare weapons and ammunition are stored in the castle, so we can arm the townsmen and hold out while the chieftain and the rest of the men are sent for."

"Can anyone get out?" Blanche asked. "They surround the castle."

"Someone must," he replied tersely. "If not, there is the risk that the Lady Fiona might ride back into an ambush."

"Who is it?" she then asked, though was not surprised at the answer.

"The Black Duncan," the man said bitterly. "He must be seeking satisfaction for the way the Macdonalds defeated the Campbells under my Lord Montrose. I heard he'd sworn then to be revenged."

Blanche stayed watching, unable to drag herself away, until she realised that she had been away from her mother for much longer than usual, and Lady Emrey might be getting anxious. She gave one last look round, and then made her way quickly back to her mother's apartments to discuss this development with her.

They saw nothing of Alexander that day, but he sent a message telling them that they were not to be concerned, the castle could hold out for a long time, and help would arrive before then.

Blanche rose early the next morning and climbed to the tower. Alexander was there, and he smiled quickly in greeting before continuing to give his orders rapidly and clearly to the men stationed on watch. She walked over to the far side to look down, but little seemed to have changed. Already there was a great deal of activity amongst the beseigers, but now the townsfolk were also working, strengthening the walls and barricading the gates as best they might with the limited means available to them. They seemed well organised, working in groups directed by the men from the castle, and Blanche assumed that this must be due to Alexander's energy. She turned to glance at him, to find that he was approaching her.

"Is your mother unduly concerned?" he asked. "I regret that there was so much to do yesterday that I did not have leisure to visit her. I trusted that you would be capable of soothing her fears."

"She is not afraid. We lived in greater danger, possibly, in England. But how will you send a message to John? How can anyone get out of here?"

"A volunteer was lowered over the walls last night, and might get through their lines. They are thinly spread, for Duncan has not all three hundred men John estimated that he would be able to raise. I count less than two hundred here."

"That is formidable enough," Blanche began to say, but her words were cut short by a trumpet blaring out suddenly from the camp.

There seemed to be a great deal of activity going on in the centre, and they realised that a procession of sorts was forming and marching towards the town gate.

It consisted of about twenty men, and they watched in silence, puzzled to discern its purpose. As they drew nearer the walls, the marchers suddenly raised long pikes, and before Blanche realised what was happening she heard Alexander's sharp intake of breath and he whirled away and was clattering down the steps of the tower.

Startled, she looked back at the fields, and now saw to her horror that on the ends of the pikes were the dismembered parts of a man, his head raised higher than the rest, in the middle of the grotesque line that had now come to a halt facing the town wall.

A howl of execration rose from the throats of the townsfolk overlooking the scene, and several of them fired muskets at the enemy, but they were too far away to be very good targets. They turned, however, and took their grisly display back towards the camp where, to the vociferous anger of the watchers, fuming impotently on the walls, they flung the remains of what had once been a man onto a fire.

"Who — who was it?" Blanche asked faintly of the man beside her.

"The volunteer who attempted to cross the lines last night," he informed her grimly. "But we'll show them, there'll be a dozen volunteers to take his place next time!"

Slowly Blanche turned away. All that day she was very silent, worrying about the difficulties of getting a message out of the town, and conjuring up horrifying visions of the inhuman vengeance the attackers would be likely to take on any they captured.

On the following day there was more distressing news. Blanche heard from the watchers on the tower that the attackers had taken hostages, young girls of ten and eleven, from a few outlying farms they had passed on their way to the siege.

"Why? For their perverted entertainment?" she demanded furiously.

"Not yet, we hear. They were afraid that someone from these farms would go to tell the chieftain and her men of their approach. It was to prevent that from happening that these girls were taken," the guard told her.

"Do they plan to subdue the town first, then wait for the chieftain to return?"

"If they can, but we are more than a match for them!" he declared stoutly.

"But if Lady Fiona rides back unprepared

she and the rest of the men will be ambushed. They can do that without first taking the town."

"Lord Alexander will get a message through, do not fear," the man asserted.

"Was someone sent to try last night?"

"Aye, this time lowered down the cliffs to the loch. Since that side of the castle is unapproachable, they have but a small contingent watching from the far side of the loch. It was hoped that by crossing to the far bank he could evade them."

That afternoon, though, it was demonstrated that he had not been able to avoid their vigilance, for a gibbet was set up in the fields facing the main gate and the man, still alive, was strung up for all the townsfolk to see.

Until this time the besiegers had done little except organise their lines. After the hanging, drawing and quartering of their victim they began to bombard the castle. Most of their shot fell short, for the castle was so high most of it was well out of range of their small cannon. During the night, while the bombardment went on continuously, they changed the target, aiming now at the town gate. Battered ceaselessly, and with fire arrows shot over the wall having repeatedly to be stamped out, the activity was frantic all through the night. Blanche was unable to sleep for the noise of the booming cannon and the shouting of the townsfolk, and went several times up to the tower to huddle in her cloak and watch the vicious attack. Twice she met Alexander, his face blackened with smoke, when he came up to the tower to view the enemy, but he merely smiled abstractedly at her and on the second occasion commented that she had best try to sleep, despite the noise.

Lady Emrey had dozed a little, and was very heavy eyed when Blanche went to join her for breakfast.

"Were any more attempts made to send out messengers last night?" she asked, and Blanche shook her head.

"I do not think so, for I have heard no reports of it. After what happened to the others I would not expect many eager to make another attempt."

"John will come back soon, no doubt," his mother said confidently.

"If he does not ride into an ambush! We must get word to him!"

"Lord Alexander will see to that, he will not be deterred by a couple of setbacks," her mother said calmly.

Blanche was not able to share her confidence, and shortly afterwards wandered up to the tower. The bombardment seemed to be lessening, and she hoped that the attackers might now have given up hope, or else be short of ammunition. When she reached the tower battlements she was greeted with an eerie silence, broken only by occasional shouts, and she soon saw the reason. The gate had been battered until it hung on its vast hinges and a fierce attack was being mounted against this breach in the defences. All the men of the town were concentrated to repel the attack, and Blanche was certain that the tall figure in the thick of the fighting was Alexander. The men, undisciplined but desperate, were holding off the attackers, but just as Blanche thought that the attempt would be repelled the cannon started booming again, this time directed at one of the small postern gates near the shore of the loch. Some of the defence had to be diverted to deal with this fresh menace.

Fascinated against her will, and with an

odd sense of unreality, Blanche watched. The enemy were again shooting fire arrows over the walls, and many of the turf covered roofs were in danger of catching fire. The defenders were fully occupied with dousing these arrows where they fell. Despite their efforts, a few fires had caught hold, but the major disaster came when the great wooden gate burst into flames. There was nothing anyone could do to prevent its being consumed, and the defenders were compelled to draw back out of range of the heat and sparks while they watched helplessly, prepared nevertheless to spring to the defence of the gap across the rapidly charring remains of the huge old gate.

Before this could happen, though, there was an unexpected development. A tall blond figure appeared on the wall above the gate, half enveloped in the rising smoke. It was Alexander, and he was waving a white flag. Blanche was horrified. Did he intend to submit to the attack? So far as she could judge the townsfolk were holding their own and could continue to do so, despite the destroyed gate.

Faintly, borne on the slight breeze, the cheers of the besiegers when they saw

Alexander came floating up to Blanche, and she raged helplessly. He was betraying Fiona and the Macdonalds who had left him in a position of trust. Mayhap, she suddenly thought, he had concerted this with Duncan for some dark purpose of his own.

From the ranks of the besiegers a squat, stocky figure rode forward on a great black horse. Even at that distance Blanche was certain it was Duncan. They began shouting, the tall blond and the swarthy, short but powerfully built Duncan, as all grew quiet about them. Although unable to distinguish a single word, Blanche realised that they were making some sort of bargain. She heard the coo of a dove as one of the castle flock flew up to the tower to perch beside her, and suddenly appreciated the silence that seemed so strange after the hours of listening to the booming of the cannon, the shouts of the fighters, and the crackling of the flames. She glanced towards the inner part of the town and her attention became riveted. Streams of figures filled the narrow lanes that led upwards towards the castle. They climbed steadily, and Blanche could see that the vast majority of them were women and children, but she could also distinguish a few men, old and decrepit, being helped along. Below her the huge gates leading into the castle courtyard were slowly swinging open, and the people began pouring in.

They hesitated at first, looking about them in a dazed manner, but the menservants down in the courtyard were directing them and they passed on towards the great hall.

"The castle will not hold everyone from the town!" Blanche exclaimed, and the man beside her chuckled.

"Have you not seen the preparations being made at the church?" he asked, and Blanche glanced where he pointed. A procession of men wound across the square outside the West Door, carrying sacks and baskets and bales of hay. The big main door was already barricaded, and they entered through a tiny side door, many of them having to put down their burdens and push them through before they could themselves enter, so small was the opening.

The man saw her puzzled look. "The

men will barricade themselves in the church after the women are all safe in the castle," he explained.

"What good will that do, when Duncan has the town?" she asked gloomily.

"Time, for he will cease attacking us while he and his troops settle themselves in the town and bring up their cannon."

"The better to be able to bombard the castle into submission," she said bitterly.

"Lord Alexander will have a plan," he replied, with such sublime confidence that she stared at him in astonishment.

"Why should you think that?" she demanded.

The man shrugged. "I was with him in the wars, and he always did find a way out," he said simply. "I confess I cannot imagine what he has in mind now, but be certain that he has a plan. He will parley with the Campbell just long enough for all to be made ready inside the town, and then we shall see!"

Blanche looked back towards Alexander on the wall. His stance told her that he was perfectly at ease, despite the difficulty of having to shout to make Duncan hear him. She noticed as she watched that several times men crept up to him, hidden by the outer parapet, and appeared to deliver messages. He never looked down at them, or back towards the town, but Blanche knew that he was fully aware of the progress being made there.

"They're nearly all inside the castle now," the man commented. "It will be almighty crowded tonight!"

Suddenly aware of the practical difficulties of housing these hundreds of people, Blanche realised that she ought to be helping, and with a last look round at the activity in and about the town, she turned to leave the tower and went to help organise the feeding of the townswomen and their children.

9

BLANCHE knew no more of what was happening outside in the town for several hours, for she was busy helping to organise women and their children, feeding them, and then settling them in makeshift beds in the great hall and many of the other rooms of the castle. The private apartments were almost the only rooms not to have several families billeted in them. When there seemed no more to be done, Blanche retired to her mother's room to find a small table set for three beside the fire.

"Lord Alexander sent a message asking if he might sup with us," Lady Emrey explained.

"What has he arranged with Duncan?" Blanche asked quickly. "Why did he give up the town?"

"That you must ask him yourself. I know nought apart from what the servants have been telling me all day. Those poor women! Tomorrow I must try and walk with a stick, to see what I can do to help."

"You are not able to yet," Blanche protested, but weakly, for she knew her mother too well. If there were unfortunates needing her help, she would do her utmost to provide it.

At that moment Alexander came in. He had found time, Blanche noted with a scornful look, to bath and change into fresh clothes. He looked immaculate, all traces of the smoke and dirt of battle had been removed. She was honest enough to be ashamed of her thoughts as she watched him bow over her mother's hand and enquire how she did, realising that if he had presented himself to her mother in any other condition she would have been even more disapproving.

He explained that he had negotiated with Duncan that the besiegers should be allowed to occupy the town on condition that they harmed no-one. Duncan had agreed to allow the townsmen to barricade themselves in the church, and the castle servants to retreat to the castle before he entered the town.

"But why give him that much?" Blanche

demanded. "He will not abide by those terms for long!"

"I am aware of that. Black Duncan is confident that we cannot hold out for much longer, so much so that he agreed to hand over his hostages too."

"The little girls?" Blanche asked quickly, a friendlier note in her voice.

"Yes," he said briefly. "We brought them up to the castle and the townswomen are mothering them. They were not harmed apart from fright. Of course Duncan only let them go because he was able to placate his men with promises of greater sport soon, but as the families of the children will not know that the girls are safe, they will not dare to send messages to Fiona."

"But how long can we hold out with them so close?" Blanche demanded. "Surely our chances are less now than they were, and we cannot send a message either!"

"Yes, there is a way, and we can hold out for long enough," he said confidently.

The food arrived then, and he refused to say anything more, pleading laughingly that he was ravenous, but promising to explain after they had eaten. Blanche waited impatiently for the last of the dishes to be cleared away, and then Alexander sat relaxing before the fire.

"What do you plan?" Blanche asked, when he did not appear to be willing to talk.

"I am going myself," he answered quietly.

Blanche felt a stab of apprehension, which she dismissed as astonishment.

"You would dare, after what they did to those others?" she asked breathlessly.

"I never ask any under my command to do what I would not dare myself," he replied gently.

She blushed, mortified. "No, of course! I did not mean that, precisely. I meant, was there any chance, any hope of escaping them? Surely now they are in the town they will be more difficult to evade? And will you not be needed here, to be in charge? What if he attacks the castle?"

"I do not think he will attempt that, for a day or so, and I have a very able lieutenant, a man who has fought with me and Montrose, who can safely take my place for one day. That is all I need to bring John and the rest of the men back."

"But why must you go?"

"I am the only one who knows the way, and so I must."

"What way? What do you mean? How do you propose to go?"

"Beneath the castle there are many old caves and passages, built, some would have it, more than a thousand years ago. Has Fiona not shown them to you?"

"Yes, some, but she said she did not like being down there, and that they went for miles and were all the same, so we did not go far."

"They do go on for a long way, but they are not all the same. They are not all natural caves. One of the passages leads beneath the town wall and further along the shores of the loch, emerging in a cave in the bank. I can get out that way."

"Why did you not use the passage before?" Blanche queried, puzzled.

He looked at her and smiled. "Until Duncan moved into the town, some of his men sat right above the cave where the passage ends. In fact, I would not have been surprised if they did not sleep in it."

"Might they not have found the passage?"

"No, it is well hidden from inside the cave. I could have held the town walls for longer, but he would have gained them in the end, and with unnecessary bloodshed. I had this in mind when I bargained to permit him to enter the town, hoping that there will be less killing and pillage. It enables me to take the message to John earlier, and when we return Duncan will be caught at a disadvantage within the town, between two forces."

"But why must you go yourself?" Blanche asked. "Why not show one of the men the way out of the castle, and let him go on from there?"

He shook his head. "It is a secret that must not be revealed to any man outside the family. I swore to my uncle, when he first showed me the way, that I would never betray it. It is not that we fear the disloyalty of our Macdonalds, but a weak man might be tortured into betraying us." Suddenly he grinned. "My uncle said nought of telling a woman. But that brings me to another favour I must beg. Lady Emrey, your son and I have not been on good terms of late, and we parted while he was most suspicious of me and my intentions. If I did show another man the passage, and sent a message that the town is taken, I fear that he would not believe me, or think that I have betrayed Fiona in order to gain control over her. He may well refuse to make her stay behind, fearing a trick, and I cannot allow her to ride into a battle."

He paused a moment, then turned to look at Blanche. "Would you dare to accompany me, to assure your brother that it is no deception, and all is as I say?"

Blanche stared at him, nonplussed, then swiftly nodded her head.

"When do we start?" was all she said, and he smiled in approval.

"Later tonight. Lady Emrey, have I your permission? I swear that Blanche will come to no harm. We will be well away from the castle before dawn, and I know where we can find horses to take us to Fiona. It is a few hours only and John can return here by mid-afternoon. Blanche can remain with Fiona at Uncle Colin's until all is resolved."

"I trust you with her. How long will it take you to get out of the castle?"

"Normally an hour. That was the time it took when my uncle first showed me the secret way. But occasionally there are fresh falls of rock, only small ones, and I may have to clear them. I want to allow three hours to get out of the castle and away from it before dawn. Blanche, if you are certain you must sleep for a few hours now, and I will come for you when it is time."

Despite her excitement Blanche did fall asleep, to be roused by her mother in the middle of the night. She donned dark, warm clothing, and was waiting when a soft tap came on the door and Alexander slipped into the room. He smiled approvingly to see her prepared, and with a few brief words of reassurance to Lady Emrey, led Blanche from the room.

The passages of the castle were lit at intervals with flares, and men patrolled. They exhibited no surprise or curiosity as Alexander led her past them, but she blushed furiously when he bent down to whisper in her ear that they probably credited him with an amorous adventure with one of the girls from the town.

"'Tis well for your reputation that your hood hides your face," he said, laughter in his voice.

"I suppose your reputation is so bad that you need not conceal yours!" she snapped, thankful that her hood also hid from him her blushes.

"Oh, past redemption," he murmured, and she determined to ignore him.

They were going downwards into a part of the castle Blanche had only once before visited. As they came to the end of a short passageway, Alexander picked up two candles lying on a small shelf cut in the rock of the wall, and lit them from a nearby flare. Then he opened a small door that led to another narrow stairway, curving as it followed the outer wall of the castle keep. He handed one of the candles to Blanche, and led her downwards again. Now they were in a rabbit warren of store rooms and the way seemed endless as they passed through rooms hacked out of the rock upon which the castle was built, and down still more steps. At what seemed to be the bottom, when Blanche thought they must be well below the surface level of the loch, they came on a series of connecting cellars with no stores apart from a few forgotten barrels or a pile of ancient logs. In one of these Alexander crossed to a barrel standing by itself in one corner, and setting down his candle rolled the heavy barrel aside. He bent down and Blanche saw a trapdoor similar to the one which had enabled her and Fiona to escape from the ruined tower. Alexander heaved on the ring and pulled up the trapdoor.

"There is a short drop, no steps or ladder," he informed Blanche. "I will go first, then you must sit on the edge and when I tell you, jump. I will catch you."

Without waiting for a reply he swung himself down, hanging for a moment by his hands before dropping into the void below. Blanche suppressed a gasp, but almost immediately his voice came floating up to her, echoing oddly as it reverberated along the passage below the trap.

"Pass me the candles," he said, and she leant over the hole to peer down at him. His outstretched hand was only half a yard below her, and by lying on the floor she was able to give him the candles which he set on a flat rock behind him.

Taking a deep breath, Blanche sat on the edge of the hole, and when Alexander gave the order, she shut her eyes and pushed herself away from the side and jumped, to feel his arms about her almost immediately. She stretched her toes out to feel the floor, but he did not set her down immediately, and, startled, she opened her eyes to find herself held with her face on a level with his, his laughing eyes close to hers.

"It is unwise to leap with your eyes shut, for you may not see where you land," he murmured, and then, before she could answer, set her down and turned away so abruptly that she almost overbalanced, and had to put out her hand to the wall to steady herself.

Her heart was beating so loudly that she was afraid he might hear it. It was not because of his nearness, and the fact that he had held her in his arms for longer than was strictly necessary, she angrily told herself, but due entirely to the fright he had given her, and the excitement of this midnight adventure.

They were in a passageway carved roughly from the rock. Alexander led the way along it. Several times they passed side openings, but he never hesitated. Sometimes the roof was so low that they had to bend almost double. The rock walls were damp, glistening with the moisture that in places ran down in tiny rivulets, but the floor was even and when they came to steps these

213

were cut shallowly and were wide and easy. Blanche exclaimed in amazement when they suddenly came out into a huge cavern, the roof high above them so that the puny lights from their candles showed only a part of the walls disappearing into the darkness.

"This is as large as the castle great hall," Alexander told her. "We need to follow this wall to the left."

"It is magnificent," Blanche said in awe.

"Aye. There are legends in the district about a hidden cave where witches meet. I've no doubt it's a memory of this cave, passed on through many generations who have had no notion that it exists beneath the castle! Some day I will bring you back to see it properly, but there is no time to pause now."

Some day. For the first time in weeks, it seemed, Blanche remembered the young man who would soon come from England to claim her as his bride. She was never likely to be down in these caves again, she thought, with a strange pang of dismay mingled with loneliness.

They entered another passageway,

narrower than the others, and it also began to slope downwards quite steeply. Alexander took Blanche's hand in his and guided her over the more treacherous, sloping, wet floor, and she was glad of his support when they came to some steep, broken steps. Once she slipped, and his arm was immediately about her, steadying her, and her heart beat fast again, while her legs trembled, in fright, she told herself.

At the bottom of these steps they found a pile of rubble, rock which had fallen from the roof and was completely blocking the way.

"It is loose stuff, I can soon move it," he said reassuringly, and began to pull aside the larger pieces of rock. Blanche set her candle down beside his and joined him, heaving at the jutting pieces of rock. He did not comment except to smile at her, and they worked side by side for about half an hour before they had cleared a space sufficiently large to crawl through.

After that the going was easier.

"We are almost down at the level of the loch. It is not far now to the cave."

In a while Alexander stopped.

"The passage twists in a yard or so,

and this cave is just round the corner. The entrance to the tunnel is high in the wall, out of sight and hidden by a ledge, but we dare not use our candles for fear someone is there. They could see the light," he whispered, close to Blanche's ear.

He blew out the candles and put them in his pocket then, holding Blanche's hand firmly and comfortingly, led her forward slowly but confidently. She felt the side of the passage with her other hand, and found herself being drawn round a sharp bend. Alexander's breath fanned her cheek.

"We must crawl the last yard," he whispered softly. "The opening is narrow and not high. Take care."

She dropped obediently to her knees, and as she moved cautiously forwards in the pitch darkness, she felt his hand on her head, protecting her from the rock that she could not see, but which she guessed hung close above her.

"Lie down and listen," he breathed in her ear, and she did so, stretched out uncomfortably on the rocky floor. All she could hear was the beating of her heart, and she thought that if there was anyone in the cave, they could not fail to hear her. But all was silent, and Alexander was evidently satisfied, for he produced one of the candles, struck a flint, and after several attempts managed to light it. As the faint glow illuminated their surroundings, Blanche looked curiously about her, realising with some horror that she was lying on a narrow ledge in front of the narrow opening of the tunnel, and the floor of the passage was several feet below them.

She shivered. One more step and they would have gone hurtling down onto the rough rocky floor of the cave. But she had no time for worrying, for Alexander was already moving and he swung himself over the ledge and dropped easily down into the cave, then turned and reached his arms up towards Blanche. She looked down into his eyes and thought that they mocked her. Flushing slightly, and recalling vividly the previous time she had jumped into his arms, she scrambled into a sitting position and again jumped down towards him, trembling to feel his warmth and strength enfold her for a brief moment before he set her on her feet.

"We are making excellent time," he

commented as he turned to pick up his candle. "Would you like to rest a while? We must set off well before dawn to be far away from the castle, but if you wish we could spare a half hour?"

Blanche shook her head. She was not tired, and in any event had no desire to wait here in the dark cave so dangerously close to the castle. She pushed aside the uncomfortable thought that neither did she especially wish to be alone here with Alexander, whose proximity she was finding oddly disturbing.

"I am not weary, and would prefer to make haste," she replied in a low voice.

"Come then. Take my hand for I must dowse the candle." She clung to him as he led the way unerringly across to the cave entrance. Although it had been cold in the caves Blanche had been too preoccupied to notice. Now, as they emerged into the open beside the loch, she shivered at the increased chill in the air. There was no moon, but the stars gleamed brightly above them, and as she looked about she could see the faint sheet of water that was the loch winding away from them. Turning, she saw the vast bulk of the castle looming above, a menacing shadow.

Alexander's voice, close to her ear, brought her attention back to the task they had yet to complete.

"The track follows the bank for some way. There is just enough starlight for us to see, but we will not be seen. Keep near the trees as much as possible."

He retained her hand in his, and she was unashamedly glad of the comfort it gave her as they began cautiously to follow the faintly visible path that edged the river. A strong breeze soon arose, and Blanche shivered and pulled her cloak more closely about her. Alexander felt the shiver and stopped, pulling a small flask from his pocket.

"Drink this, it will warm you."

Blanche took the flask, and gasped as the fiery spirit flowed down her throat. It stung, but immediately she felt the warmth steal over her.

"Thank you," she murmured, and Alexander put the flask back in his pocket. He slipped his arm about her shoulders and held her close for a moment.

"We walk for perhaps an hour, to where

I have a friend who will lend us horses. Come."

He urged her forward, and she went as though in a dream. It must be the effects of the whisky, which had been very potent, she decided, as she appeared almost to float along supported by his arm. The dream was shattered when Alexander suddenly halted, and then pulled her down behind a tree, his hand firmly clamped over her mouth. Startled, she began to struggle, but he held her with ease and bent to breathe in her ear a warning that they had almost stumbled over a sentry post.

Instantly she lay still and he took away his hand. They had been observed, however, and a challenge rang out. When Alexander remained silent they heard a swift muttering barely two yards ahead. Then cautious steps came towards them, and Alexander stood up, so silently that Blanche felt rather than heard his movement. As the sentry approached he shot out his hands and grasped the man, twisting his arm so that the dirk he carried fell harmlessly to the ground. The man let out a cry of alarm, swiftly choked off as Alexander plunged his sword into him, so that he dropped soundlessly to the ground.

The warning had been given, however, and Blanche heard the steps of more men thrusting through the undergrowth towards them. Terrified, Blanche thought the noise must come from at least a hundred men, and she crouched where Alexander had pushed her, straining to distinguish the shapes that loomed formlessly in front of her.

As the man he had killed dropped to the ground, Alexander had turned to face the rest of the attack. There were two of them, but they hesitated to attack, unaware of how many opponents they faced, and in addition wary of hitting one another or their comrade who was before them.

Alexander, unable to see more than vague shapes that appeared more solid than the surrounding darkness, slashed and thrust indiscriminately. Soon there was a gasp of pain that told him one of his opponents was hurt, and he almost fell over the man who was rolling on the ground in his agony. Alexander leapt backwards, knowing that his remaining opponent would be at less of a disadvantage. Giving way slowly, able to see the deadly sword only by the occasional flash as the starlight was reflected on it, he moved towards the waters of the loch. Enticing the sentry by appearing to be afraid to attack, he drew him on until, as the man lunged forwards, he stepped swiftly to one side and smiled grimly at the splash as the man hit the icy cold water.

Moving quickly and competently, he pulled thin, strong twine from his pocket, and as the man's hands appeared, clutching at the edge of the bank, he tied them together, laughing softly as the helpless man cursed him. Then he hauled the fellow out and similarly secured his legs. Next he dealt with the wounded man, tying him firmly after roughly bandaging the wound in his leg. Blanche tore a strip from her petticoat for the bandage, and watched unflinchingly in the light from Alexander's candle as he trussed up the man. The third man was dead, the sword having penetrated his heart, and they left him alongside his companions.

"I was careless," was all the comment Alexander made as they set off once more. "I had not expected Duncan to be efficient enough to post sentries so far away. One constantly needs reminders not to underestimate one's enemy."

"Will there be more?" was all she replied.

"I doubt it, but we had best go silently."

They met no more sentries, and as the first faint rays of light illuminated the sky, came to a largish farmhouse with many other buildings scattered about it, barns and sheds and cottages. Alexander led the way to the door and hammered on it, and a window above the doorway was flung open.

"What the devil is that? Who makes that unholy row?" a man's angry voice demanded.

"The devil himself," Alexander answered, laughing, and the man above gave a cry of welcome and disappeared, soon to be unbarring the door and effusively inviting them in.

"Alex, my dear fellow, what brings you here at this unearthly time?" he asked, and glanced fleetingly at Blanche. She blushed as she read the speculation in his eyes.

"No time to explain. I need horses. Duncan has attacked my cousin and possesses the town. I must ride to Fiona and fetch the rest of the men. She is with Colin."

The man wasted no time. Shouting for his servants to bring wine and some slices of cold beef, he nodded to a settle beside the fireplace.

"Sit there for a moment. The lady goes too? While you eat I will see to the horses, and I will ride with you."

Alexander did not attempt to argue, seeming happy to allow his friend to make the arrangements. He led Blanche to the settle and flung himself down beside her.

"Fergus Macleod was my friend when I was a boy, and since then we have fought together. He is utterly to be depended on. We will eat while he deals with the horses."

Blanche found that she was hungry, and did justice to the food a goggling maid soon set before them. They had barely time to eat the beef and some cold chicken, the whole washed down with an excellent wine, before Fergus was at the door with his horses. Alexander lifted Blanche into the saddle and they rode off, the story of the siege being told to an angry Fergus as they went.

"'Tis unbelievable that no word of this should have reached us! We are so near!"

Alexander explained tersely how the silence of the farmers about had been obtained.

"Duncan needs a lesson. I am with you if you will accept my assistance!"

Alexander laughed. "With the greatest of pleasure," he replied. "I hoped you might join me in this fight!"

The journey to Colin's house was accomplished with no more incidents. It was just after mid-morning when the three of them rode up to the strongly fortified house. They were challenged by a man on duty at the gateway.

"At least Fiona seems well guarded here," Fergus commented as the man, recognising Alexander and Blanche, bade them welcome and offered to conduct them to Sir John.

"He insists on seeing all visitors personally," the man explained rather apologetically, but Alexander laughed.

"Good. I want to see him without delay."

After his first surprised greetings, John listened intently to the story Alexander had to tell, turning unconsciously to Blanche for confirmation. Alexander's lips curled wryly and he met the apologetic glance Blanche threw across at him with a sardonic smile.

"You will believe your sister?" he asked quietly and John, too worried to see the implications of this question, nodded abstractedly.

They all went to Fiona, Alexander demanding from an incensed Katriona, avidly curious at this sudden visitation, that they speak in private with his cousin. Fiona appeared and courteously but firmly dismissed her aunt. Such was her dignity that although she grumbled, Katriona recognised defeat and went. Then the story was related to Fiona and John, who had been busy making his plans, detailed them to her.

"You will have to stay here. I can leave only half a dozen men, those I can trust, with you. I will take your uncle and as many men as he can provide with me. That will be safest. We should reach the castle in time to give battle before dark.

Tomorrow, or as soon as it is safe for you to return, I will send for you."

Fiona shook her head. "I am chieftain and I will ride with my clansmen," she said calmly.

They stared at her in amazement.

"Do not be so ridiculous," Alexander broke the silence, but Fiona turned on him angrily.

"My father and his father before him led the clan into battle. I will do no less."

"But you are a woman, not fitted for such a task," Alexander retorted.

"I may be a woman, but I am subject to no-one. If I choose to do something, you will not deny me!"

John stood up slowly and looked down at her, then took a deep breath.

"If you insist on putting yourself into danger so, my lady, then I can no longer serve you as your steward," he said, the words dragged painfully from him.

Fiona stared at him, aghast. "John! You would desert me?" she whispered at last.

"No, never!" he uttered in agony, looking down into her eyes turned beseechingly up to his. "My bounden duty is to protect you, and I cannot permit you to take such a risk. If you were hurt by any negligence of mine I could never live at peace with myself again."

For a long moment Fiona stared back at him, and then she lowered her gaze.

"As you wish it, John," she said simply.

10

JOHN had leapt into furious activity, hurling orders at his men, and within a remarkably short time the Macdonald clansmen were preparing to march. Fiona stood on the steps of her uncle's house and watched as they went past, led by John. They cheered vociferously as they marched past her, waving their bonnets, and she watched, tears in her eyes as she waved back. Blanche stood at a window and watched her brother as he led the way out of the courtyard. Then her eyes turned to where Alexander, with Fergus and Colin and his men rode in the rear. She had had no words alone with anyone since that extraordinary scene when John had forced Fiona to his will, and she was still somewhat bemused by the meek capitulation of her friend. Alexander had been immersed in the preparations, and Fiona had gone to talk with the men as they saddled their horses and loaded up what little baggage they proposed to take with them.

Blanche looked on as the last of them disappeared. They would make good speed for most of them were mounted and the others could, she knew, maintain an incredibly fast pace. Also they had no heavy equipment to slow them down, for they had no big guns to take. It had been decided that a swift battle was the best way to defeat Duncan, since they had no means of mounting a siege, so the few pack ponies carrying food could follow more slowly. She turned to go to the room Katriona had given her when she had heard the story, but she had scarcely reached it when Fiona came bursting in, the calm she had displayed for the last hour deserting her.

"Blanche! I cannot bear it! He might be killed! I must know, I must, I tell you. I cannot wait for them to bring him back to me. I am going after them. Will you come with me?"

Blanche stared at her in amazement. This wild girl was so unlike the normally calm and dignified Fiona she knew that she had no answer to give apart from a weak protest.

"You cannot! You promised John."

"I said I would not ride with them to lead them into battle! I did not promise that I would remain here, helpless, awaiting news of what happens!"

"That is but a quibble," Blanche retorted, recovering her wits. "He was worried for you and would never forgive me if I allowed you to run into danger."

"I will be in no danger, Blanche, I swear, for I will keep well back from the fighting."

"What if they lose?" Blanche asked bluntly. "If they do not defeat Duncan you will not be able to escape."

"If they lose I know John will have died. He would never run away. And if he is dead what have I to live for?" she asked, almost in tears.

"The clan, your lands and your family!" Blanche declared bracingly.

Fiona shook her head. "I care for nought of any of it if he is dead!"

Suddenly the tears welled over, and she clung to Blanche. The younger girl drew her to sit on the bed, where she put her arms about her friend and comforted her as best she might. Gradually Fiona's sobs lessened, and she sat up, wiping her eyes, and smiled bleakly.

"You must think me a fool to give way so, but I love him so very much!" She stood up. "Thank you, Blanche dear. I would not drag you into danger but I am going."

"Then I am coming too," Blanche replied. She had done her utmost to dissuade Fiona, but she was in just as great a turmoil of mind, anxious to know the result of the battle and the fate of those involved. Not even to herself did she admit that it was Alexander's fate that concerned her most.

Fiona gave her a dazzling smile, and they went to order horses to be saddled. The six men John had left behind as a guard for Fiona were horrified at the very thought, and only gave in to her when they saw that unless they used force to detain her she would go without them. They did not dare treat their chieftain so, and therefore grumblingly made ready, with many loud comments that their lives would not be worth a moment's grace when the steward discovered their disobedience.

"'Tis rank mutiny," one of them muttered loudly enough for Fiona and Blanche to hear as he mounted.

"Nonsense, Jem! I order you, and can

order my steward," Fiona said coolly, and turned her horse to lead the way, watched by Katriona, half anxious that she would be blamed, but half hoping that ill would come of it.

Most of the way was through wooded valleys, not so narrow or so wild as those Blanche had struggled through on foot after the abduction. Surrounding the town there was a narrow ring of cultivated fields which had been cut out of the forests, and the castle on its hill rose majestically at its centre, the loch curving protectively about the base.

With the shelter of the forest hiding them from watchers in the town the clansmen were able to approach the town to within half a mile before they needed to leave cover. In the edge of the forest John formed them into companies and then, on a signal, they marched out on a long front, trumpets hurling defiance and pipes wailing as they advanced straight for the town.

Fiona and Blanche, with their small, worried escort, had remained just out of sight of the marching army on their journey, and as the clansmen spread out across the fields they moved cautiously to the edge of the trees, keeping within their shelter and out of sight.

On the ride Fiona had talked quietly to Blanche, admitting to her that she had been in love with John since she had first met him.

"If Patrick had not been killed and I had married him as my father wished, that would merely have seemed the destiny of one in my position," she explained. "I could have borne it. But with his death all has changed. I hate the thought of making a loveless marriage by my own choice, and yet what alternative is there? You must know your brother, Blanche. Do you think he has any affection for me?"

Blanche stared at her friend, astonished that she could not see what was so plain to the rest of his family.

"Of course he loves you!" she exclaimed. "Do you not know that from the way he looks at you, the way he wishes to do everything for you, and waits on your every word?"

Fiona smiled, and then spoke somewhat tremulously. "I had wondered, I had hoped, but I thought that I might be pretending, reading into his politenesses more than was meant!"

"You probably read too little!" Blanche declared.

"Even so, would he ever consider asking me to marry him?" she asked wistfully.

"I think he would consider it presumptuous," Blanche had to admit. As Fiona nodded, her eyes bleak, Blanche continued: "But the marriages of girls such as you are arranged through third parties much more than those of ordinary folk. You could, with all propriety, ask him. Apart from your feelings, would the people accept him? He is an Englishman, and landless so long as the King has no power."

"If I married a Highland chieftain the clan would lose its independence and become part of another clan, and so they would prefer John for that reason. It was one thought in my father's mind when he arranged the marriage with Patrick. My relatives would howl in dismay, of course, but the ordinary people love me and would be delighted that they would see a love match. It would be on my part, but can I be utterly certain of John?"

"What do you mean?"

"How could I be certain he loved me? I know that he has great regard for me, and from what you say I begin to hope it is more than that, but I must be sure! You see, he is so noble, he might feel obliged to accept, so as not to hurt me, were I to propose to him!"

"I doubt if he would do that even if he did not love you," Blanche tried to reassure her friend. "You worry over nothing."

"But he may love someone else? Is there anyone?" she asked slowly.

"No, and so far as I know there never has been. If he has contrived to hide from you his love it must be because, thinking marriage impossible, he has tried to push it from his mind."

"I wish there was a way to be sure!" Fiona exclaimed in agony. "I am too proud to beg him, and would feel too humiliated if he agreed without loving me. Has he ever hinted at the idea?"

"Not directly, but being John he would not. He does not show his feelings too openly."

Fiona rode on in silence while Blanche, full of pity for her friend and her brother, was busy planning ways in which she could herself act as an intermediary. But all these plans were dismissed from her mind as they watched the men in front of them form up, and then spread out on their approach to the town. They heard the shout of triumph rise from two hundred throats as the men of Duncan Campbell's clan poured hurriedly out of the gateway, bereft now of its gate, and prepare to face the far smaller number of attackers.

From the castle itself came a fusillade of shots as the defenders, seeing deliverance at hand, defied their besiegers and attempted to catch them between two fires.

Implacably John, his men, and those who had accompanied Colin marched forwards. The men without horses formed a solid wedge of infantry in the middle of the line, and their mounted comrades rode on either wing. Before the Campbells had time to form the cavalry on the left, led by Alexander, charged along the bank of the loch, breaking into a canter and sweeping round in a graceful curve to gallop alongside the walls of the town, thundering down onto the disorganised beseigers turned defenders.

As they swung round to face this menace,

a volley of musket shot crashed into their ranks from John and his men in the centre, and many of those that were left whole turned to flee from the loch and the town, and straight into the charge of the other wing of cavalry.

Duncan's men were not all craven, though the unexpectedness of the attack and its force had thoroughly demoralised them. As a small group stood fast together and cried out angrily to their comrades, many of the confused men rallied again and returned to the fight. After such a charge Fiona's men had little opportunity to form up again, and the battle developed into hand to hand fighting as the Macdonalds sought to capture the enemy, who wanted only to escape from the trap they were in. A few of them, realising that they had been outmanoeuvred by the surprise, saw a chance of escape and broke out of the mêlée, running as fast as they could for the shelter of the forest. Only a few were mounted, for the attack had been too sudden to permit them to lead their horses from the town, but one of these, a broad shouldered, powerful looking figure, suddenly broke away from the fight and galloped away, his spurs cruelly raking his horse's flanks.

"'Tis Black Duncan, after him!" The cry rose from so many throats that Fiona and Blanche heard it even over the tumult of the fighting further back.

He had a good start, and once into the shelter of the trees might yet escape. His pursuers, John amongst them, were far behind.

"Head him off!" Fiona ordered swiftly, and her men, who had been fretting at their inability to join in the battle waging before them, needed no further urging. They set off, streaming towards the flying figure as he headed for the refuge of the trees to the side of them. Fiona, heedless of her own safety, forgetting all in the need to prevent the escape of this man who had dared to attack her people, rode after them, and Blanche with her.

Espying this new danger, Duncan swerved in an attempt to avoid the men pounding towards him, but they were too close and had soon surrounded him and dragged him from his horse. Spluttering curses, he stood there glaring venomously at Fiona, who had reached the group with Blanche just

239

behind her. She was about to speak when her name was called, and she turned to see John ride up to her.

"In God's name what do you here?" he demanded furiously. "I gave orders — "

"John, you are wounded!" she cried, and slid from her horse's back to run towards him.

Holding his left arm, which was bleeding profusely, away from him, he dismounted stiffly and took a step towards her. Blanche, slightly behind Fiona, saw a movement from the corner of her eye as Duncan, attention momentarily distracted from him, drew a pistol from its holster and raised it to aim. She screamed a warning a second before the pistol was fired and gasped as Fiona, running towards John, fell to the ground. John leapt across the small gap separating them and dropped down beside her.

"My love, are you hurt?" he asked in an anguished tone. "Fiona, my dearest one!"

After what seemed an eternity to John she opened her eyes, and a sweet smile curved her lips as she looked up at him.

"I but tripped on a tussock and winded myself," she said with a faint laugh. Then she noticed the blood on the sleeve of his coat and sat up swiftly. "You are hurt!" She threw a glance over her shoulder and gave swift instructions to her men. "Secure the Black Campbell, I will deal with the fiend later. Fetch help for Sir John, quickly. Make haste, I say!"

She did not look closely at them, her whole attention being concentrated on the task of easing off John's coat, and did not realise that one of the men, reacting to the firing of the pistol beside him, had turned and driven his dirk into Duncan Campbell's heart. Blanche saw their looks of astonishment as the prisoner they held sagged and collapsed to the ground, and she quietly went across to them and suggested that they remove him, and explain what had occurred later when Lady Fiona was more at leisure to attend them. Nodding thankfully they agreed, and looking about them saw that the battle was virtually over, only a few isolated struggles still taking place.

The remnants of Duncan's army were soon rounded up, and the townsmen, released from their enforced vigil in the church, set to with a will to dig a grave for the ones that had perished. The church became a hospital, and the wounded, mostly Campbells, were carried in to be tended by the women who had been driven by them to take refuge in the castle.

John's wound was not serious enough to incommode him once it was bound up, and despite Fiona's urging he insisted on remaining on the field to direct the clearing up. Meekly she accepted his order to take charge in the castle and remounted her horse to ride in what proved to be a triumphal progress through the town. The castle cooks were busily preparing a banquet to celebrate the victory and the children, catching the exhilaration of their elders and wild with pent-up emotion after days of fear, were busy gathering a huge pile of rubbish and wood to build a bonfire in the church square.

Fiona sent for John as soon as it was reported to her that he had returned to the castle.

"Did you mean what you said when you thought I was hurt?" she asked shyly.

"I must beg your pardon, I ought not to have said such things," he answered with difficulty, keeping his eyes fixed on hers.

She smiled. "I am glad I fell, glad that Duncan tried to shoot me, for you revealed your heart. John, I must marry, but I will marry a man I love and who loves me. Do you love me enough to share my tasks?"

His look answered her, and with a glad cry she went into his arms. Much later she recalled that she ought to be preparing for the banquet.

"I shall announce our betrothal tonight, before you begin to think of all the disadvantages," she said gaily.

"Your family, ought they not to be consulted?"

"I will inform them, but not consult with them," she said firmly. "I am their chieftain and shall do as I wish. Besides, Colin has departed already to return to Katriona, and there is only Alex here. The others have had no care of me."

"You are too fierce, my love!" he chided gently, and as he pulled her towards him she melted, soft and submissive as she held up her face for his kisses.

Blanche and Lady Emrey were told beforehand and gave their wholehearted approval. Alexander, having been in the thick of the fighting without suffering a scratch, had been with the clansmen until just before the banquet began, and joined Fiona and the Emreys as they were about to enter the great hall. Fiona stopped, drew him slightly to one side and told him her news. Blanche watched anxiously to see how he would take this destruction of his own hopes.

"Wish me happy, cousin?" Fiona asked him, a challenging look in her eyes.

"I have not always appreciated Sir John, my love, but I think he can master you!" he said, and laughed at the look of indignation that crossed her face. "Marry him soon so that he can have the task, thankless as it is, of guarding you!"

"I will do so," she replied softly, and passed into the hall with John.

When the announcement was made, the wild cheering rang all through the castle, and the word spread faster than fire down the hillside into the town. Soon the castle gates were besieged by the townsfolk calling for their chieftain and the popular Sir John. There was no doubt as to the view of her clan.

Fiona and John went hand in hand to walk in the town, to light the great bonfire, and to receive the warm congratulations of the people. Lady Emrey, whose leg was still painful, retired to bed and Blanche went to help her. As she emerged later from her mother's room Alexander rose from the windowseat where he had been waiting.

"The best view of the celebrations is from the tower," he said, holding out his hand.

As if she had no will of her own Blanche allowed him to lead her up onto the tower. Far below them the streets were ablaze with torches and flares, and lesser bonfires had been started as well as the great one before the church, so that the town looked as if it had been visited by an army of gigantic gloworms. They could see the people dancing in the streets and squares, and the singing was borne up to them on the breeze.

Blanche looked further away from the castle. Beyond the lights of the town, the fields and the forests loomed darkly, with the only brightness the silvery twisting loch winding away towards the sea, between the rough, afforested hills. Suddenly she thought of the man who was coming to carry her away from all this, and a silent tear fell onto her hand. How could she bear to go back to England, away from this land and these people she had grown to love so well, even though it meant returning to her old home.

"Are you sad for your brother? Surely not!" Alexander's voice startled her. She had not realised that he had been watching her. Embarrassed, she turned her face away, but he took her chin in his hand and forced her to turn her tear-stained face up to him.

"What is it?" he asked, and without conscious thought Blanche stammered that she did not wish to leave the castle.

"I shall miss it so! " she said with a catch in her voice.

"But you will not be far away, and can visit your mother and John and Fiona frequently," he said bracingly.

She stared at him, frowning slightly. "England is a long way," she whispered.

"You can visit there too, if you so desire it."

"Visit? But I shall be living there!"

"What do you mean? Surely your mother

does not plan to return now?"

"No!" she said desperately. "Roger Grant lives there."

"And who might Roger Grant be?"

"The man I am going to marry," she answered dully.

Alexander gave a shout of laughter, and she looked up at him angrily.

"I can see no cause for merriment," she said furiously, and turned to run towards the door of the tower. But he was after her in a single stride, caught her and forced her to turn and face him.

"Have you ever met this man? Do you love him?" he demanded, and helpless in his grip she shook her head.

"It is being arranged," she managed to say.

"Then it can be disarranged, for you are not leaving Scotland. You are going to marry me."

Bemused, she stared up at him, thinking that possibly he was unhinged over his disappointment that he would not now marry Fiona, or had some plan of revenge on John through her. Then a strange emotion seemed to overwhelm her, there was a tingling in her limbs, and his face seemed to be coming nearer, his eyes devouring her.

"I — I do not understand," she whispered in a trembling voice.

He chuckled. "Surely you know what marriage is, my lovely one? Or shall I explain? It usually begins when I pull you close to me, my arms imprisoning you so that however much you resist, you cannot escape. Then there is a kiss, timid and afraid of a rebuff, like this. Later the lovers grow more expert, and the kisses are more like this. Yes you learn fast, my beloved. You begin to return the embraces, your arms about my neck, so, and becoming more daring, your arms cling to me more fervently, more surely. That is right, my darling. You respond to me, not because it is an arranged marriage and your duty, but because you love your husband with all your heart, as he loves you. I do not think I need explain any more to you!"

There were no more words as he clasped her to him, and Blanche, ceasing to wonder how this thing had happened, how this love that she had not dared admit even to herself was, miraculously, returned, submitted joyfully to his caresses.

"I thought you wanted Fiona," she whispered, a long time afterwards. "I thought you meant to rule her clan."

"I often thought of it while I was away fighting," he admitted. "It seemed sensible. But then I did not know that you existed, and once I had set eyes on you there was no other remotely possible course of action. I do not often confess to being incapable of controlling my actions, but since I have met you I have had one main objective, to make you my wife. I could not, even if I wished, fight against that. It is our destiny, and I suspect it is the same for John and Fiona."

She smiled at him shyly. "They are deep in love," she said, almost apologetically.

He regarded her with amusement. "If he had not loved her, do you think I would have permitted their betrothal?" he asked, laughing, and she laughed joyfully back at him.

"I would have liked to have seen you trying to restrain Fiona once she was determined to do something," she replied teasingly.

"She will be an excellent chieftain, and John will be able to guide and help her.

She will do what he wishes, despite herself, just as I fear you will be able to rule me, my enchantress!"

"It must be a dream!" she said suddenly. "I shall wake and find it all vanished!"

Gently he kissed her again. "No, my sweet love. It is reality, a reality better far than any dream."

THE END